IT'S
OVER

LAURA L. SMITH

Birch House Press
Est. 2015

It's Over

Copyright © 2013 by Laura L. Smith

Cover Design ©2013 Angela Llamas Photography by: Kelci Alane Photography

Scripture quotations in this publication are taken from the following: the *English Standard Version*. Copyright 2001 by Crossway Bibles, a division of Good News Publishers. *The Message* by Eugene H. Peterson. Copyright 1993, 1994, 1995, 1996, 2000. Used by permission of NavPress Publishing Group. All rights reserved.

It's Over Status Updates Series (Book 2) / Laura L. Smith. – 2nd ed.

ISBN-13 9780996277006

First printing 2013

Printed in the United States of America

[1. Romance—fiction 2. College—fiction 3. Roommates—fiction 4. Christian life—fiction 5. Death—fiction]

Birch House Press
Est. 2015

For my brother, Jim, who will never understand how tightly I hold on to the string that tethers us together

CHAPTER ONE – KAT

AS WE TURN ONTO MY street, my eyes are transfixed by the alternating blue and red lights coming from my driveway. My roommate Palmer places her hand over mine, but I can't register why. Why would there be a police car at my house?

"That's weird," I mumble.

"It's all right. It's probably nothing." Palmer's voice shakes a little. Why does she sound nervous?

"Wonder if the neighbors are all right?"

"The cops are at *your* house," Palmer whispers.

We park, get out of the car, and walk in slow motion up the driveway, past the flashing lights, past the static of police radios. Palmer carries my laundry bag as I lug a duffel bag and my backpack to the front door.

"Sorry, miss, you can't go in there." A burly policeman with a brown bushy moustache blocks my way.

"I live here," I manage to mutter through the lump in my throat.

"Wait here." Moustache Man stares straight ahead.

"What am I waitin' for? It doesn't look like he's doin' anything," I squeak to Palmer.

Daddy's Rav4 races up the driveway. His tires squeal like a NASCAR speedster, and he springs out of the driver's seat—so not normal for Daddy. He's usually really calm, in control.

I look to Palmer for some explanation of the *Twilight Zone* scene. Palmer's chocolate eyes shine. She shakes her head.

"Where's my boy? Where's my wife?" Daddy's voice bellows as he sprints toward us, almost knocking Palmer and me over with his tall frame. "Kat?" he whispers, straightening me like a book he's knocked off a shelf, placing his strong hands on my shoulders, but just for a second.

"Are you Mr. Wiley?" the policeman-turned-bouncer demands.

"Who do I look like? Of course I'm Mr. Wiley!"

Everything's turned inside out. Something is so terribly wrong. Goose bumps climb up my calves. Tears scald my eyes.

From somewhere inside the house comes a shrill cry. What is that? Is that Mama? Daddy charges past Moustache Man to the sound of her wails. I try to follow, but the policeman grabs my arm a little too hard.

"My mama needs my help!" I fight to get free. His grip remains firm and burns my bicep.

"Hey!" I try to swat him away.

"We're helping her, miss. You'll have to wait. Your dad's with her. After my partner talks to them you can go in." The policeman's voice sounds like it's coming from a swamp—dark, muddy, and gurgly. Nothing he says makes sense. None of what's going on makes sense. I bang my head against his navy blue chest like a football player charging the other team, but he won't budge. I bang and I bang and I bang and I bang, until I can't lift my head another time. I collapse against his stone-hard chest, not caring about his sharp badge poking my forehead or the stale smell of cigarettes lingering on his shirt.

"C'mon, Kat." Palmer's voice punctures the dark cloud encasing my body. "Let's wait over here."

Palmer must have the remote control for my body, because I can't make myself move, yet I end up on our porch swing, swaying back and forth, holding her hand, staring at the flashing lights.

I never thought I'd be friends with someone like her. Rich. Gorgeous. You know the type. I met Palmer—Hannah too—when I first moved to Ohio last year. They were inseparable BFFs at the high school I transferred to. When we found out we'd all be attending Clarkston College in the fall, we decided to be roommates. Add Claire, the ballerina from Cleveland whom Hannah met at orientation, and we're oddly a perfect fit.

I notice how cold Palmer's manicured hand feels against my hot, sweaty one. The continued glare from the top of the police car gives me something to focus on. I don't know if I sit here for a minute or an hour or a week, but eventually Daddy's in front of me, blocking my view of the blue and red streaks.

"Kat." He puts his strong hand on my shoulder.

I look up, trying to focus but can't shake the blurs of light from my brain. I find Daddy's straw-colored hair and bright green eyes among the streaks of light, and then the rest of his face comes into focus. Mama swears my brother, Alex, looks exactly like Daddy did when she met him. But right now Daddy's face is twisted, like it's made out of Silly Putty.

"Alex was in a car accident." The words drop like bowling balls on a wooden lane, crashing and echoing, then rolling forward faster and faster as they barrage the row of neatly placed pins, sending them flying in different directions before they crash to their sides.

"What happened?"

"I don't know." Daddy covers his face with his enormous hands. He stays covered up for what seems like hours. The police walk out of the house, right past us with just a nod, and head back to their car.

The slam of their doors snaps Daddy's attention back to me. "He was on his way home from the pool and another car came around the corner." Daddy shakes his head in disbelief. "They say the other driver must have never seen him." He clears his throat and continues, "The police came here to tell Mama. All they had listed was our phone number from Nashville, but they got our address from Alex's license plate. Mama called me."

The cops pull out of our driveway, almost silently. My eyes follow them disappearing into the dusk.

"Where is he?" I ask, searching Daddy's face for answers to the questions too painful for me to form, too impossible to ask.

"He's at Mercy Hospital in ICU." Daddy's gaze is somewhere above me, and his voice is whispery, like a cloud I can stick my hand through. "There's internal bleeding. They're doing surgery."

"We have to go." I grab Daddy's arm. "Get Mama."

"What?" Daddy clears his throat. "Right, let's go."

"Oh, Kat. I'm so sorry." Palmer hugs me, her Burberry perfume surrounding me. "I'll be praying for Alex and for you. I'll text Hannah and Claire. Let me know if there's anything I can do, okay?"

I hug her back, afraid to let go, afraid of what will happen if I emerge from the perfume cloud and let the next play of this awful game begin. If only she *could* do something!

"Make this all a dream," I say. "Or . . . or," I choke, "make Alex's surgery go all right. I need the best surgeon in the world. Pray for the best surgeon in the entire world," I blurt, releasing her and turning to look for Daddy. He's gathered Mama into his car and is getting in. Did they forget about me?

"I'll take you," Palmer offers and grabs my hand.

CHAPTER TWO – HANNAH

"HANNAH BANANA!" DAD GIVES ME a big old bear hug. I drop my bags on the ground to hug him back. Since our dorms have a keycard system, I meet him in the turn-around in front of the building.

His arms feel warm and safe like a sleeping bag. I could crawl inside and crash for a while.

"You traveling light these days?" Dad raises his eyebrows and laughs.

I have a roller bag, a large duffel, and my backpack crammed with gear for my three-day fall break.

"You should have seen how much stuff Palmer took home. She had at least three suitcases, her makeup bag, her jewelry bag, a crate full of shoes—she said she's trading out her summer shoes for winter ones. You should have seen Claire's face when she asked her how many pairs of shoes she had and Palmer answered, 'I have no idea.'" I blow a bubble with my gum for emphasis as Dad pops his trunk and sets my bags inside. "It's a good thing you could get me on the way back from Cincinnati. I might not have fit in Palm's car."

"It worked out great. I knew I had to have lunch with someone from this account at some point. Why not today?" Dad turns the key in the ignition, bringing his old BMW to life. "So, how's college treating you?"

"Oh my gosh, where do I start?"

I talk the full two-and-a-half-hour drive home about my classes and boys and campus and the food at the dining hall. I explain how I'm thinking about trying out for this girls' a cappella group called the Songbirds next week and that I've started taking spinning classes at the fitness center.

As Dad pulls into our driveway, I stop talking for a second and just look. This is my first time home since school started. It's like all the things I was talking to him about are in one world—a faraway world called college. And this place, our stucco house with gray shutters, is another world, the one I actually live in. I take it all in— from our mailbox stenciled with flowers, to the golden mums on either side of the front step, to the mat that reads Welcome by the front door. Tension I didn't even know I had around my nose and behind my ears softens.

As soon as we pull into our garage Ziggy, my golden retriever, Sammie, my twelve-year-old sister, and Owen, my eight-year-old brother, come tumbling out the door. They tackle me as I get out of the car, all ruffly heads and gangly arms and waggly tails. Well, Ziggy's the only one with a tail.

"Hannah! Hannah! Hannah!" my brother and sister chant. Ziggy barks.

"Do you like my sweatshirt?" Sammie asks, swiveling her shoulders to show off the lavender hoodie with Clarkston stitched across the front.

"You look absolutely adorable, Sam. I love it!" I squeeze her.

"I begged Mom and Dad for it, because I'm going to go to Clarkston too."

"You have to. It is so fun and the campus is positively beautiful, and there are millions of cute boys everywhere you look."

"Come see my new Lego set." Owen tugs my arm. "I built it all by myself."

Ziggy circles me, around and around, making sure I won't leave.

"How d'ya do your hair like that?" Sammie eyes me.

I nod to Owen while rubbing Ziggy's silky head. "Sure, O. Just a sec." And then say to Sammie, "Umm. I'll show you. Palmer taught me with the curling iron. She's amazing with hair and makeup and clothes, which was always a plus as a friend, but as a roommate it's the ultimate."

"Come on, Hannah." Owen tugs more insistently. "I've been waiting a-l-l day!"

"Sure. Sure." I look to Dad to see if he needs help with my bags.

"Go ahead." He laughs.

I practically trip over my flats as Owen pulls me into the playroom and Ziggy darts between and around us.

"Hi, sweetie!" Mom intercepts Owen by hugging me, her chunky sweater embroidered with autumn leaves and acorns cocooning me. It even smells like home here —vanilla bean candles and lemon furniture polish.

"Hi, Mom." My eyes tear a little. I didn't expect them to. I love college.

I do.

But maybe I didn't realize it, until just now, but at school I'm constantly trying. Trying to be the perfect roommate. Trying to pull all As. Trying to find a boyfriend. Trying to look the part. Trying to do all of that and make it look effortless.

Three minutes back at home, and I'm bombarded with people trying to love and impress *me*.

"It's good to be home," I say quietly, because I'm afraid if I speak too loudly my voice will crack and Mom will think something's wrong.

"M-om!" Owen whines. "I'm trying to show Hannah something."

"Of course, Owen. He's literally been checking the clock every couple of minutes since he's been home from school."

Ziggy barks, making sure I don't forget her too.

Owen grabs my hand and pulls me toward the table where he does all his building. "Wow, Owen. What a cool set! Is it Ninja dudes?" I sit down on the floor to let him know I'm giving him and his creation my full attention.

"Yup. Ninjago!" His eyes light up. "And the master lives here and their weapons are here and this door here, see? It opens like this. And these are their spinners. This is the coolest guy, the guy in red."

"Awesome. I love red, very sharp. If I were a Ninja, I'd want to be the red one. What's his name?"

"Kai."

"Owe, this is really cool. You are an awesome builder."

"You're an awesome sister." He snuggles onto my lap, which he hasn't done in ages. His body is warm and seems to fit with mine just like two connected Legos. "Will you stay at home now?"

Ziggy finally settles down and plops next to us, guarding us, thumping her tail on the floor.

"She'll stay for the weekend." Mom shakes her head so only I can see. "Speaking of, what are your plans?"

"Nada. I want to eat real food, sleep in, and maybe go shopping?" I plead with my eyes. "Pretty please on the shopping. I really want some boots, and I need some stuff for school. I have a list."

"That all sounds doable." Mom nods. "Tomorrow can be a sleep-in day, and we can hit the mall while the kids are at school. O has a soccer game on Saturday. He'd love for you to watch him."

"I'm the goalie!" Owen squirms in my lap.

"I bet you block all the balls," I say.

"And," Mom says, "we promised Grampa a visit on Saturday too."

"Great." I pick up a Lego guy and attach him to a spinner.

Owen twirls him like a top. "It works like this."

Mom taps me on the shoulder. I look up, and while Owen's face is engrossed in Kai spinning in circles, she mouths, "We need to talk about Grampa."

CHAPTER THREE – CLAIRE

SOMEWHERE ALONG THE FIVE-HOUR bus ride, the wheels of the Greyhound thudding along the highway from Clarkston College to Cleveland lull me to sleep. I wake to the lurching of the bus as it makes a tight turn along the exit ramp. *East of Eden*, which I'm reading for English, is still open on my lap. The noxious exhaust fumes make me a little queasy, or maybe that's because in the commotion of traveling I skipped lunch. I grab a granola bar I snagged on my way out of the dining hall this morning out of my backpack and peel back its wrapper.

Definitely not the most glamorous way to travel, but for $35 with my student discount, it's hard to beat. I would have had to fork over that much in gas money to someone on the ride board to get home for fall break, and I'm not that hip on riding anywhere with strangers.

I nibble on the end of my bar, swallowing sticky oats and raisins as the bus sways off the exit ramp and into the streets of Cleveland.

At the bus depot riders mechanically unload, one after another, leaving seats, grabbing gear. All I have is my purse and a tote bag jammed with a few textbooks, a couple of outfits to swap with Mom, and my laptop.

Outside the station, it's just a couple steps to the city bus stop, where I'll grab another bus to take me to my apartment building. The aluminum seat sends a sharp shock of cold along my rear as I sit. I pull my long sweater closer to my body to fend off the chill in the gray fall air. I slide my sunglasses over my eyes, although it's not bright enough to warrant them. From behind the big lenses I can safely scope out my surroundings.

An old woman sits on the bench next to me. She seems harmless enough. Two younger guys with black hair, both wearing gray hooded sweatshirts and ultra-low-riding jeans, chatter in Spanish in the corner of the glass bus shelter. I dig in my bag for my perfectly faded denim jacket I scored at a thrift store and slide it on for extra warmth.

"This bus takes longer and longer every day," the old lady says in a gravelly voice.

I nod and smile tight-lipped, not wanting to engage in conversation. My eyes shift across the street, sizing up the people walking back and forth. I glance at the baggy-jean boys. They seem innocent, but I don't trust people these days. Not since Paris. Not since Phillip.

I gently pull the bobby pins out of my bun, letting my curls tumble along my back.

Phillip.

His name makes my heart shriek. Phillip, who seemed like the boy of my dreams, who seemed like my Prince Charming until he forced himself on me, stealing so much. Uneasy, I stand. Two middle-aged men in coveralls join our group. I step around them, to avoid being trapped between them and the other woman.

Our bus groans as it comes to a stop along the curb. I let everyone else get on first so I can pick my seat. The thick exhaust tastes toxic on my tongue. I climb into the bus, quickly assess my options, and walk down the aisle.

I pause as I pass the old woman, but decide on an empty window seat near the back.

I can't get home fast enough.

Maybe I should have ridden with someone from Clarkston, a college student, someone from my school, instead of a sea of strangers. But no. I knew Phillip. Knowing someone doesn't mean you can trust them. Knowing someone doesn't make them safe. My fingers shake as I slip in my earbuds and play Matt Brouwer's "I Shall Believe."

"*I know it's true, no one heals me like you*," he sings, reminding me of what I tend to forget, reminding me God is with me on this journey, this bus trip, always. I close my eyes, reminding myself, I. Shall. Believe.

Going to college so soon after the rape, the day after I landed back in Ohio from Paris, was a shock to my system. I thought it would be the way out for me. A new place, new friends. And in a way it is. My roommates, Hannah, Palmer, and Kat, crack me up. They're patient with me. They comfort me. They help me be stronger. They insulate me with their friendship. But now I'm headed back home. Not that it happened here, but home is where Mom is. And Mom, although she loves me and has spent her life trying to do what is best for me, is the fragile, insecure adult woman I most fear I'll become, the antithesis of who I want to be when I grow up. When I'm around her, I feel her frailty. It pulls me toward it. It frightens me.

Off the bus, I walk on autopilot down the streets of my neighborhood. Sirens wail. Cars squeal to stops. Cigarette smoke spirals from neighbors I've never met, and garbage rots in nearby dumpsters. These familiar sounds, sights, and scents are oddly comforting.

The heels of my cowboy boots clack past the skate punks doing jumps on their makeshift ramps in front of my building. Avoiding eye contact with any of them, I turn the key in the glass door, quickly and deliberately. Once inside, I bolt the door and climb the stairs to the fourth floor.

"Hi, Mom. I'm home," I say, swinging the door to 4C open.

The apartment is dark and empty except for the lone bulb burning over the kitchen table and a pile of cardboard boxes stacked precariously by the door.

CHAPTER FOUR – PALMER

THROWING MY CAR INTO PARK and snatching my bags, my fingernail snags as my hand catches on the door handle. I rub my thumb over its jagged edge. "Crap!"

I sprint inside to be welcomed by the soft light of our great room and the sweet smell of apples and cinnamon floating through the air. I exhale for the first time since I left Kat's.

"Hi, hi, hi!" I say, trying to sound normal, but not liking the tinny sound of my voice as I set my bags by the staircase.

"Palmer Ruscilli!" Mom peeks out from the kitchen island wearing a cashmere sweater and black slacks.

"You're here!" I say, hugging Mom tightly, clinging to the solidness of her body and the softness of her sweater.

"Of course I'm here." Her laugh seems to say, "Silly girl."

"And I made the apple crisp. A promise is a promise." She leans back and looks at me, raising her eyebrows. "Look at you! Have we maybe gained a few pounds? Too much dorm food? Maybe a smaller portion of apple crisp?"

I suck in my stomach, momentarily distracted from my panic. "I don't know . . ." I look at the oven longingly. "But, Mom, that is so *not* the point! I am totally freaked out!"

"It barely shows." Mom smiles, turning back to the island where she opens a bag of pistachios, their bright green screaming against the black granite counter.

"The freak out or the pounds?"

"Stop." Mom waves her hand. "What has you in such a state of drama?"

"It was horrible!" I shout, sitting on a bar stool next to the island, but my knees can't stop bouncing up and down. "When we got to Kat's house, the police were there! Her brother was in a car accident! Bad. I think it's real bad."

"What happened? Should we go over there? How far is their house from here? Do you need to go to the hospital?" Mom drops the towel she was folding.

"I was just at the hospital. Can you believe it? It was crazy weird. Her parents were completely out of it. So I drove Kat to the hospital and sat with her while they figured out where they were supposed to wait and who they needed to talk and all that. What if he dies?" I shake my head. "What if it had been Kat or Tia or me? I can't even get my head around it."

The tears I held back to be strong for Kat, to get myself home, roll down my cheeks. "I texted Claire and Hannah to let them know and then drove home, like, in a total daze. For a second I had that freaky feeling you wouldn't be here." I exhale. "I'm so glad you're here. And everything's okay, and mmm, that apple crisp smells amazing." I sniff.

"Are you all right?" Mom comes around the island and hugs me. We stand there for a minute. Me trying to breathe like a normal person. Mom propping me up. "Honey . . ." She leans back and brushes my hair out of my face. "I have to pick up Tia from tennis in about half an hour." I feel her body tighten as she cranes to see the clock. She exhales loudly. I don't need Mom to fret about her schedule. I need her to worry about me.

"I don't want to leave you here by yourself. Do you want to come with me?" She rubs my arms.

"I . . ." I try to breathe deeply, like in yoga, to calm myself. "I just want to be here. Home."

Mom gives me an extra squeeze. "I know."

She looks back at the clock, then again to me. "I guess you could call Keegan, so you don't have to be alone." She says the words with such strain in her voice, I know this is her last resort.

Mine too.

Keegan's name makes me suck in my stomach again, to try to get rid of the lurching feeling down there. I haven't seen my boyfriend, if he even still is my boyfriend, since the first weekend of school when I came home to visit, which started out lovely and ended in a screamfest.

Mom knows some of the story, but not everything. Not the "Keegan's livid because I'm not ready to have sex, even though he's so darn sex-y" part. I don't think she could handle it. I know I can't.

The timer beeps. Mom eases the apple crisp out of the oven. Thick and syrupy apple juice bubbles from the oatmeal crust. I sigh, allowing the sweet, homey smell to soothe the mayhem of my thoughts.

I grab my phone and text Kat.

You ok?

No. But praying for miracles.

Me too. Want me to come back and sit with you?

No. Still in surgery. Nothing for you to do. I'll keep you posted.

"No news. I'd be a wreck." I set down my phone.

"You are a wreck." Mom looks at me, putting her hot pads back in their drawer.

"Thanks." I nod with a giant fake grin, signaling I don't appreciate her sarcasm, especially at a time like this. "Kat and her parents are just sitting there at the hospital while her brother is in surgery. Can you imagine just sitting there? They need prayers big-time." I pause, wondering how much to share with Mom about Keegan. "Mom, you know Keegan and I are a mess, right?"

"Of course, but I'm sure if you needed someone with you, he'd jump at the chance to be here. I thought you had plans to see him while you're home."

"Thunder!" I squeal.

Thankful for the distraction of my kitty strolling nonchalantly toward me, I hop off the stool and scoop her up, stroking her fluffy, gray fur and nuzzling her sweet, impish face. "You always know when Mom's cooking, don't you, Thunderkinz?"

"So, do you want to call him?" Mom asks.

So much for distractions. Thunder jumps out of my grasp and scampers out of sight. I grab a pistachio and slide my burgundy shellacked nails along the slits at the top. I really need a nail file. "No. I can't. I'm too freaked out. We're supposed to see each other tomorrow. Supposedly. But I'm pretty sure he's still mad."

"Of course he wants to see you. You're the best thing that ever happened to him. And he's jealous, dear, not mad." Mom shakes her head as if it's all so obvious. "You are clearly going to the better college. You have a plan for your life, and he's just playing baseball at Polaris State. It's not like he's going to be a professional athlete." Mom rubs a fingerprint off the stainless steel fridge. "Not to mention his classes started a whole month after yours. By the time he left home, you were already involved at Clarkston. Long distance is tough, dear. Maybe there's someone else out there for you. Like a smart, rich Clarkston boy." Mom wipes the counter.

She never really liked Keegan. She's fine with him as a person, because he's always polite and well-mannered in front of her, but not as my boyfriend. She says he won't be able to provide me with the life I'm used to.

Do I even want that life?

Do I even want a life with him?

I used to think I knew everything I wanted. Now I don't feel like I know anything I want.

"Tell me about some cute boys at school."

Ding-dong.

"I'll get it." I jump at the chance to escape Mom's line of questioning.

I tug on the brass handle. Keegan's intense gray eyes stare into mine.

CHAPTER FIVE – KAT

WE SIT AT THE HOSPITAL for hours. The three of us stare at the greenish gray walls, inhaling the scent of antiseptic and burnt coffee while listening to the shuffling of soft, squishy nurse shoes. I flip through every old issue of *People*, *OK*, and *Sports Illustrated* on the table, but can't keep enough focus to actually read an article. I kind of wish Palmer would have stayed, but what good would that have done? I twist the silver rings I've acquired at various art festivals around and around my fingers. I text Palmer, Hannah, and Claire to give them the update—the update of not knowing anything.

At first, messaging my friends helps me feel connected to them, like I'm not completely alone. But after back and forthing with lots of questions from them and no answers from me, I feel even more desperate and unable to control what's going on. I click off my phone, unable to tap out another round of "IDK" and "No news."

Mama, Daddy, and I sit and shift on uncomfortable chairs for more than three and a half hours, learning nothing more than when we first arrived. Alex's car got hit—make that totaled—as he made his way past an intersection on Summitt Street. Alex was alone in his car. Two Ohio State boys, where Alex goes to college, were in the car that hit him. They're fine, basically, some cuts and bruises, a broken arm, or was it a wrist? I can't remember. They might have been high or drunk. But that's all speculation. All I know is they're at home and we're here at the hospital, watching reruns of *Everyone Loves Raymond* on the small, square screen mounted in the corner of the waiting room.

Alex has been in surgery for as long as I can remember existing.

I don't know if we first hear the doors open or see the doctor in her teal scrubs and skullcap, but Mama, Daddy, and I jump in unison. The surgeon walks slowly, deliberately, tilts her head and sighs, not a sigh revealing any emotion, just a sigh showing her exhaustion.

"You are the Wileys?" Her voice is solid, matter of fact, but her eyes look tired.

"Yes." Daddy's the only one who manages to find his voice.

"Alex made it through the surgery."

A shrill, nervous laugh escapes Mama's candy-colored lips. She lives by the mantra that Southern belles should never be caught without lipstick. Everyone says I look exactly like her, minus the lipstick. I know they're comparing our matching straight, dark brown hair, mossy eyes, fair complexions, thin frames, and even twin moles at the corner of our right eyes, but still I cringe a little at being compared to a forty-eight-year-old who dresses exclusively from Chico's and wears bright pink lipstick.

The doctor doesn't smile, but continues in a monotone, "He made it through, but his injuries are severe. He lost consciousness upon impact and has not regained it. He will be in ICU overnight and tomorrow. If he's strong enough, we'll undergo the second surgery. He lost a lot of blood."

"Can we see him?" Daddy asks.

The doctor shakes her head.

I look to Mama and Daddy. I can usually read from their faces if something is wrong, the way Daddy's jaw tenses and loosens, a certain light in his eyes; the way Mama's eyebrows arch, how her shoulders scrunch or roll back.

Daddy's jaw is tense. Mama's shoulders are as rigid as a hanger. The phrases "second surgery," "ICU," and "lots of blood" bounce around my head.

"I suggest you get some rest. I know it's been a long day for all of you. You're welcome to make yourselves comfortable here. Someone should stay close."

"I'm stayin'," Mama says in her nonnegotiable tone.

"Good." Daddy swallows hard and looks at the ceiling while he slides his hand around her back. "You think maybe I should take Kat home?"

The doctor gives a tight smile, nods, and pulls out a stark white business card. "If you need anything or have any questions, I'm on all night. If you can't find me, you can call my cell." Her stubby fingers with nails clipped short point to the bottom of the card.

"Thank you," Daddy says.

The doctor nods again, turns, and walks silently away.

"You wanna go home . . . ?" Mama's eyebrow twitches as she looks at me. I can tell there was supposed to be more of that sentence, but Mama swallows and lets out a low, racking sob.

Daddy holds her for a long time. I stand there, watching my mama fall apart on my daddy's broad shoulders, imagining my brother with tubes up his nose and wires on his chest and not being able to do anything, not one thing.

Then Mama grabs me and strokes my hair, like she did when I was little and I'd sit in her lap. "I love you, baby," she says.

I long to stay here in Mama's arms. I don't want to let go.

"I love you too, Mama."

And then we both remember that I'm eighteen and we untangle ourselves, but I can't let go. "I'm stayin' too."

Mama shakes her head.

"We'll all stay together," Daddy insists. "That's how it should be."

CHAPTER SIX – HANNAH

MOM SITS NEXT TO ME on the couch. I shift a little. I'm stuffed from the steaks Dad grilled and Mom's famous Death by Chocolate.

"Just a sec. I need to finish this text to Kat." I type the last word and push Send. "I am over-the-top worried about her. Please keep her in your prayers. She's really gonna need them."

"Did you say her brother was in a car accident?"

"Yeah. Can you imagine?" I chew my gum. "She's not texting back." I shake my phone as if it will magically respond for Kat. "Earth to Kat, come in Kat-a-tat-tat," then set it down on the coffee table neatly stacked with *Better Homes and Gardens*, *Forbes*, *Seventeen*, a Lego catalog, and a scattering of coasters.

"So I need to tell you about Grampa," Mom says as she pats her hair.

"What about him? What's going on? Is he okay?" I turn so I face Mom. An ache spreads from my nose out and under my eyes.

"He had a fall last week." Mom bites her lower lip. "He slipped on his kitchen floor in his condo and broke his hip. They took him to the hospital and put a pin in and he's healing nicely, but he can't get around, clearly, so he's at a nursing home while he does physical therapy."

The ache spreads from under my eyes back to my temples. "Oh my gosh. Is he okay? What do you mean 'can't get around'? Is he in a wheelchair or crutches or what? And why didn't you tell me?"

Mom exhales. "A wheelchair. I knew you had an exam and a paper, and I didn't want to upset you." She takes my hand. "And they don't really know anything yet. I knew I could get you all caught up when you came home this weekend."

"Who's 'they'? And what do they not know? And do you trust them?" I chomp furiously on my gum, as if I chew fast and hard enough I'll hear something hopeful.

"'They' are the doctors at the nursing home who are overseeing his PT. And they're just not sure how he'll get around after this. He's older and his bones are brittle and take longer to heal, and he's so stubborn."

I pop my gum. "He is stubborn."

"He's not exactly what you would call cooperative in therapy, and if Grampa doesn't do all the exercises, they're worried about what kind of mobility he'll have long term."

"You mean he won't be able to walk? Like, he'll be in a wheelchair forever? That would totally stink."

Mom nods, then shakes her head, then nods again. "He'll probably always need a walker or a wheelchair or both, and he probably won't be able to live by himself anymore."

I straighten a magazine that's a little out of place. I stack the coasters neatly, enjoying the thick clink of ceramic against ceramic. "So, not living alone, what does that mean? Who would live with him? I still get to see him Saturday, right?"

"Of course. He's counting on it. Saturday is trick or treat at the senior center." Mom forces a laugh. "He's staying at the nursing home for another week or so, so he can do physical therapy and they can keep an eye on him, but they're going to transport him and some other patients to the senior center for the party."

"The nursing home?" I feel my eyes widen. "You can stay there just a few weeks and then leave? Who knew? And trick or treat at the senior center? Halloween isn't for three weeks."

"Right, but this way everyone's grandkids can come and it doesn't interfere with real trick or treat. I guess they've made it a huge community event."

"Okay," I say slowly. "Sounds kinda fun, right?" I try to convince myself.

I'm afraid of old people.

Not all old people. Not ones I know, like Grampa, just old people in general, especially when they need help, like ones at the nursing home, like when there's lots of them all in one place. I don't want to be scared of them. It's not something I've ever told anyone. It's embarrassing, mortifying, actually. I mean, I love to help people—my little brother and sister, my roommates. I live for that. But old people are grown-ups, and it seems all backwards that they need help with things like walking and going to the bathroom and remembering. I'm close to hyperventilating just thinking about spending a day with dozens and dozens of seniors.

"I know how close you are to Grampa." Mom rubs my knee, thinking all my concern is for him, which is fine, because it should be, and it mostly is. "It's just so much safer for him at the nursing home for now. Where people can keep an eye on him, make sure he doesn't fall again, make sure he's recovering properly."

"Does he feel safe there? 'Cause I don't know if I'd feel safe if someday my kids told me I had to go stay with a bunch of old people wearing diapers. And about the Halloween party. Please tell me I don't have to wear a costume." I do bug eyes at Mom in mock horror trying to lighten my mood.

"Sammie and Owen are going to dress up. That's up to you." She smiles and pats her hair again.

"I'm going to do what?" Sammie asks, strolling in wearing pj pants and a cami, suspiciously similar to my own ensemble.

"Wear a costume to Grampa's on Saturday," Mom says.

"Right. I'm going to be a beautiful witch." My sister twirls around and cackles, "Ha, ha, ha."

"You want to wear my glitter makeup?" I ask, already knowing the answer, but not expecting the full shriek.

"Oh my gosh, really?" She jumps up and down and claps her hands. "That would look so cool!"

"There's only one condition." I smile. "You'll have to share your candy with me."

CHAPTER SEVEN – PALMER

KEEGAN'S HANDS ARE SHOVED IN the kangaroo pouch of his sweatshirt. He stares at me with those droopy, puppy dog eyes of his.

Even from here, I can smell him—a kind of soapy, rainwatery, mouthwashy smell. The scent clings to his sweatshirt—the sweatshirt I've cuddled up with countless times, the same one he let me borrow when he went on a weeklong baseball tournament last summer. I wore it every night, burrowing into its softness and the scent of him while I slept.

My heart twitters. Crap. I plant the heel of my boot deeply into the plush carpet to ground myself. He smells so good and looks too good. I inhale and square my shoulders.

"Hey," I say.

"Welcome home." Keegan's lips curl into a smile and he reaches for me.

Despite my resolve to be strong, I'm so drained after being in the hospital with Kat that I throw my arms around him, snuggle into his height and warmth for some sense of support. He feels solid and safe and calms that shaky thing that's been going on in my chest since we saw the police car in Kat's driveway. But in his arms, I also remember our last conversation. I pull away.

"Speak of the devil." Mom puts on her hostess grin as she greets Keegan. "Leave your shoes by the door, dear."

Keegan slides off his gym shoes with his opposite heels. "Hi, Mrs. Ruscilli. How are you?"

"Fine, thanks," Mom says stiffly. "I'm off to pick up Tia. You need anything, Palm? Maybe some Diet Cokes?"

"No thanks, Mom." Doesn't she know the artificial sweeteners in Diet Coke actually make you hungrier? Despite my lingering resentment at her earlier fat comment, I squeeze Mom tightly, gripping her soft suede jacket. I need to cling to something, and I know better than to let it be Keegan. Don't I? I don't want Mom to leave, because I have this weird fear something might happen to her while she's gone. Not to mention I am so *not* ready to be alone with Keegan. I'm clearly not as strong as I thought.

"I'll be back in a jiff." Mom waves.

Keegan and I stand with an awkward two feet and no words between us as Mom's shoes tap down the hall.

At the click of the door, I inhale and take a step backward, trying to regain my ground and my cool and my personal space. Keegan pulls his hands out of his pockets, shakes his head, and says in his deep voice, "Wow. You look great."

"Thanks." There's a twitch in the back of my throat. I'm glad I wore my best jeans and this cashmere scarf, even though I was just driving. I didn't expect to see Keegan until tomorrow, but a girl should always look her best. This is proof.

"So, what are we going to do, Palm?" He walks behind me and wraps his arms around my waist, making me feel small and protected, encased in his six-foot-three athlete's frame.

Instinctively, I lean back into his warmth, holding on to his arms. His sweatshirt is soft and familiar, like the safe parts of what we had. "I don't know." I shake my head, because I truly don't. "I don't know."

"I miss you." He burrows his face along my neck, moving my hair out of the way, and kisses the sensitive spot behind my ear. His lips on my skin send a shiver down my neck and through my sleeves.

"I miss you too." A tear escapes the safety of my eye and spills down my face. "I think that's the problem, Keeg." I turn. "I miss you like crazy. I miss us, what we had, but I'm so confused by everything. I don't know what's left of us anymore."

He pulls me down onto the couch. I allow myself to sink into the smooth leather cushions.

"Sorry." I sniff. "I am a total mess. Kat's brother, Alex, the swimmer, remember, from OSU? He was in a car accident. Kat's at the hospital right now. I just got back from there. He might die! Die! As in dead." I swallow a large gulp of air, sit up a bit taller, and continue, "You know how much I hate to drive, and I'd driven all the way from Clarkston to Kat's house, then I took her to the hospital, and then like a spaz I finally drove home, and my mom—" I catch my breath and start to say, "Called me fat," but I don't want Keegan to even consider me being fat, so instead I say, "She was just, you know, being all my momish, and totally didn't understand. Then you show up, and you do understand, but you're mad at me." I lean back into him, trembling at my unexpected outburst of words and tears. I look away.

"It's been crazy. This whole long-distance thing," he says softly. "It's way harder than I thought it would be."

I wipe more tears and nod. "Way harder."

"I thought we'd both be busy with classes, and I'd have baseball. You know we're already training every single day, lifting and stuff, and we don't even play until spring?" He rubs my knee gently.

"Right. I know." I pick up where he left off, finishing his thought. "I knew we'd be busy with our normal stuff and see each other when we could, just like we always have. But there's a major disconnect." I let my head fall against his chest.

"So, Kat's brother, will he live?" Keegan changes the subject, but that's okay. I need to talk about both things, about Alex and about us. Right now they seem like two necklaces all tangled together. I need to pull a little piece through here and loosen a knot there to get them apart, to make sense of any of it.

"I don't know. He's in surgery. That's all anyone knows . . ." My voice trails off and I sink deeper into him, in the physical sense of letting him engulf me like a bean bag chair, but also in the relational sense of trusting him and easing up on the hurt that's been festering. I think back to the nasty accusations from Keegan the last few times we've spoken. He's been insensitive and unsupportive about school and sex and everything. Blaming me. Turning it all on me. But when I'm snuggled up with him, it feels like it was just a big misunderstanding, like when we're together everything's okay.

Say you're sorry, I will him. *If you say you're sorry for what you've said, for how you've acted, I could forgive you. Maybe everything could go back to normal.*

Instead of answering my silent wish, Keegan leans forward and brushes the tears from my eyes with the back of his hand, calloused from swinging a wooden bat over and over. Then, enveloping me in his rainwater scent, Keegan's warm lips land on mine like pillows of comfort, soft and sweet.

CHAPTER EIGHT – CLAIRE

"OH!" MOM GASPS.

I spin around. She's right behind me, arms full with her purse and school bag and Chinese carryout. Hooray!

"Mom." I grab the Chinese and her purse and carry them to the counter.

"I meant to be home before you and surprise you with egg rolls." Mom smiles, but her light blue eyes look defeated.

"My favorite, and you did surprise me." I stick my nose in the bag to see what else she ordered. "I just got here."

"Really?" Mom raises her eyebrows.

"Really. See, I'm still wearing my jacket."

"Oh." Mom scans me up and down as if she's not so sure. "All right, then." She shakes her head, and her golden hair, the same as mine, only shorter, swings around her face. "Let's start over. Walk out the door, okay? Pretend you're just getting home."

"Okay."

I walk out the apartment door and count to sixty to give Mom a minute to be less flustered. This isn't the first time I've had to pretend to help Mom feel better about something.

I open the door. "Mom, I'm home."

"Claire!" She runs to me, her sweater dress itchy as it brushes against my cheek. "Guess what—Golden Wok for dinner! Welcome home!"

"Oh, Mom," I fake gush. "I missed you."

We pull out all the food and get settled at the table. I dunk my egg roll into bright red sauce, sweet and tangy on my tongue. Mom pours us tea, and I ask about her students. She asks me about the dance troupe I made at school. I fill her in on my roommates, and she describes the new Algebra teacher at her high school who never takes off her coat and wears rain boots every single day.

"So strange rain boot teacher is new," I say in between bites. "Any other new teachers this year? Any men? Cute men who want to date an English teacher who suddenly finds most of her evenings and weekends free since her daughter is off at college?" I raise my eyebrow like Palmer would do. It's funny how little pieces of my roommates are rubbing off on me.

Mom sets down her chopsticks. "No one at school."

I take a sip of warm tea. "No one at school, but . . . someone. Do tell."

"Well, there is a greeter at church who always talks to me, but I can't figure out his story."

"Who?"

"His name is Joe, and he just moved to town. He jumped right into service. He's been a greeter the last four Sundays at the side entrance. You know I don't like the main entrance, always so congested."

"What's he look like?" I scissor my chopsticks back and forth, something Mom taught me to do when I was eight or nine, and grab a piece of chicken and a slippery carrot from my Moo Goo Gai Pan.

"Oh, you know." Mom tilts her head. "Tall, brown hair, medium build . . ."

I continue eating, that granola bar on the bus was hardly filling. After a few more bites I look back at Mom, wondering when she's going to continue.

"Mom," I prompt.

"Oh, sorry, I just . . . ," she says in her sing-songy voice. "Joe wears crisp polo shirts and well-ironed khakis, very neat and tidy looking. He's always friendly. But, after Arnot, I don't think I'm ready to jump into another relationship. Everything with him felt so right, and when he took us to Paris, I thought it was the real deal."

You think every guy is the real deal, I think, but I say, "It was quite a deal for him." I tuck my stray curls behind my ears so they don't dangle into my food. "He got to have his wife waiting for him at home *and* take you to Paris. Have you heard if she dumped him?"

Mom taps her spoon against her teacup. "No one I know has the scoop, and I don't have the guts to ask around. How about Arnot's sleazy nephew?" Mom brings up the elephant in the room. "You doing alright with what happened with Phillip?"

I wish I could spit my rice out, but it's halfway down my throat. It clogs my voice. I can't answer.

"Are you okay?" Mom asks, putting her tiny hands flat on the table. "Are you choking?"

I shake my head. Every time I get away from the rape, even if it's for ten minutes of Mom and me chatting over Chinese, it always comes back, again and again and again. I look away. My eyes fall on the boxes by the door. I'd forgotten about them in the midst of our "I'm Home" game.

"What are all those boxes for?" I squawk, sipping my tea, trying to regain my voice and my airway.

"Oh." Mom clears her throat, all fake and strange. "I . . . well . . . since you're not here in the apartment with me anymore, I'm moving."

CHAPTER NINE – KAT

BACK IN OUR SEATS, WHICH remind me of a penalty box, I cave into exhaustion, laying my head on the metal arm of my chair and curling up in a ball. I imagine the *beep-beep-beep* of the machines, which must be attached to Alex. I picture a red dot jumping up and down on a black screen like a racquetball bouncing again and again off the back wall.

But somewhere in the deepest darkest corner of the night, I hear silence. Deafening silence. The beep stops. The red light turns off.

And I know.

I know, and I sit straight up and my stomach does a flip. I see it in my head, a big red, squishy blob literally turning over in an oozing heap. I feel the thud of my stomach as it lands upside down, then something bounces and climbs up my throat. It is round and wet and gray. I feel it moving up my chest and struggling with the thinness of my throat before escaping my mouth. A sob, dense and eager to be free, shatters the silence.

There are voices and feet in soft-soled shoes and the doctor again, putting her hands on Mama's and Daddy's shoulders.

"I'm sorry." The doctor seems to speak in slow motion. "There was too much internal bleeding. We couldn't save him."

Mama's cries and Daddy's moans mingle with the background of the hospital into white noise so loud I can't listen.

I tune out the sounds and focus on the lights. I stare into the fluorescents until they have no outline, just whiteness. I feel like I'm being pulled into them, sucked into their nothingness, their emptiness.

The lights disappear, and for me, the world goes black.

I don't know how long I stay in pitch darkness.

"Kat!" Daddy's voice sounds far away, and I don't even try to answer. I don't ever want to move again. It's peaceful where I am. I could stay here. But then Daddy's shouting, and his strong fingers press too hard in my arm, shaking it. I glare at the space where he must be, hoping he'll stop and leave me alone. His face, all twisted and pink, materializes through the fog.

"It's time to say good-bye." His words sound garbled.

It takes all my energy to process what he's saying.

"Mama's in there. I . . . I already went." He swallows hard, curls his lower lip over his top lip, and looks at the ceiling. I wonder if he, too, is drawn by the lights. "Do you want to see Alex?"

Seeing Alex is all I want to do. This alone gives me strength to nod and stand. My legs feel like rubber bands bending and waving under my weight. I need to talk to Alex. He's the one I confide in. He helps me through the rough spots, and this is by far the worst thing that's ever happened to either of us. Maybe if I talk to him it'll be all right.

From the doorway, it seems Alex might be asleep, just lying still on the hospital bed, his head resting in

Mama's lap. But as I get closer, the mirage of peace is destroyed. Mama is hunched over the shell that used to be Alex. Stark white wrappings slant across his forehead, covering his left eye. Sheets are pulled up, flat and stiff, almost to his neck. His left arm is in a cast, tucked too tidily outside the covers.

But through the bandages, I catch glimpses of my brother. His rough fingers, always ready to toss a ball or shove a sandwich in his mouth, peek from behind the plaster. Despite the pink cut through the top right corner, the lips are Alex's lips. I imagine them cracking a smile or teasing me. His right eye is closed, as if in slumber, but his thick blond eyebrow bleached from chlorine knits above it. I know under the gauze on the other side is its twin, always ready to arch in disbelief or amusement. I imagine how he'd look without the bandages, but he'll never be without them. Never.

"Al," I whisper, squatting near Mama on the bed. My hand shakes uncontrollably as I touch his forehead. His skin feels all wrong, static and cold like a football, not like my brother. The tears pour. They pour down my face and they pour and they pour and they pour, and I can't stop them from coming, because I ache all over and I can't make them stop.

"Alex, what's going on?" I ask. His green eyes, the one physical trait we share, will never look at me again. How am I gonna survive without those eyes?

"Where'd you go? Why'd you leave me? Don't you know I need you? We were in this together. We were in on everything together." I choke on sob after sob reverberating from my inner core.

I don't know how long I wait for an answer before I hear the doctor's voice, like a robot, saying, "It's time now."

I ignore her and so does Mama. We sit, touching Alex.

"Excuse me, ladies. We need you to leave the room," a male nurse announces.

"I'm sorry," says the doctor, moving toward us.

"You can't leave me now! I *need* you!" I beg Alex as the doctor's hand tugs gently at my arm. I let my fingers graze his cheek as I reluctantly back away.

Daddy must have come back into the room because he lifts Alex's head off Mama's lap. I watch him holding my brother's face in his giant hands for a moment before gently laying it down.

"Good-bye, son," he whispers almost inaudibly.

Daddy puts an arm around Mama's shoulders and pulls her up, hooks my arm with his other hand, and steers us both away from the bed. As the door swings behind us, I feel an invisible string between Alex and me being stretched thinner and thinner.

The door clicks shut, but our connecting thread is stretched so thin, it fits through the crack between the door and the floor. I see in my mind Alex's hand with the scar on his pointer finger unwinding the ball of string, allowing plenty of slack for us to stay connected—no matter what.

The hallway grows longer and longer with each step, like we're walking on a treadmill. I have to force my leaden legs to take the next step.

"It doesn't feel right to leave him here," I squeak.

Mama wails and shakes, only moving forward because Daddy propels her out the door.

"He's already gone." Daddy puts his other large hand in the small of my back and guides me down the hallway step after step after heavy, laborious step.

CHAPTER TEN – PALMER

KEEGAN KISSES ME AGAIN AND again. I feel that tingle in my throat, pulling me closer toward him, into him. His hands shift down my sides and rest on the curves of my hips. I suck in my stomach, hoping *he* won't think I've gained weight. I brush my lips against the prickly stubble on his chin and give him a series of quick kisses in a line leading to his ear allowing me to whisper, "I love you."

Keegan presses into me, against me, pinning me safely between the cushion and his chest. I surrender to the dizzy feeling of dark swirls in my head and wet, warm kisses on my mouth. I love this feeling. I could get lost here. His hands slide up and down and one slips between my legs. It feels like it's on fire, even through my jeans. I squeeze my legs together. I can't stay here. I must stop being here.

"No." I push back. "Keegan, we can't."

"Why not?"

"Mom and Tia will be back any minute. Are you crazy? I don't even know where we stand." I breathe deeply, trying to escape fantasyland and return to reality.

"You just said you loved me." Keegan leans back in.

"I do." I frown. It would be so much easier if I didn't.

Keegan's lips are all over mine again, and his hand fumbles with the button at my waist.

"Stop." I pull my lips away. "Stop."

"Palm, you said there was a disconnect, but if we made love, we'd make that connection. It would keep us glued together even when we're apart. It would fix everything."

Would it?

What if we're falling apart—breaking up—and we go ahead and have sex only to end up with nothing?

I open my lips to speak, but he kisses them again. He nibbles teasingly with his teeth, lightly. "It kills me when you say no," he purrs.

"Keegan." I sit up, tugging my sweater back where it belongs. "This is so not easy, but I'm not ready. Remember? We've been through this." I feel my pulse racing. How did I let myself get swept into the thrill . . . again?

He is thrilling. *Grrr*. I clutch the nearest pillow.

"Why are you saying no, when we need this more than ever? It's like you're hitting me over the head with a bat, Palm? If you don't want me, just say so!" He rubs his hands over his buzz cut. "Don't tell me you love me and get me all hot. What's with that? You can't have it both ways." He looks down, shaking his head like Mom does when she's disappointed in me.

I'd been planning what I'd say to Keegan when I finally saw him face-to-face for weeks. I have several different speeches rehearsed in my head. But none of them started like this. It never got tangled up like this in the versions I imagined. I hug the pillow to my chest, guarding my heart.

"I'm not saying no to us. Just to sex."

"But sex joins people. It's like you're saying no to being mine. Who is it down there at Clarkston you're staying available for?"

I squeeze the silky chenille pillow tighter. "It's not like that. There's no one." I wipe another tear. My face must be a mess. "No one but you."

"If there's no one but me, then why won't you commit? What are you waiting for, Palm? Some rich boy driving a Beemer who will fit right into the mold Mommy and Daddy made for you?" His voice grows louder, edgier.

I cower into the couch. "I don't like it when you get angry. It scares me," I squeak.

Keegan stands and paces. "I wouldn't be angry if you were being true, Palm. I don't even know why I'm here. I don't know why I keep trying. All you do is slap me in the face."

He stomps to the door. He's talking, well, shouting, but it seems more like Keegan's spitting a bad taste out of his mouth. "Forget it. It's over, Palmer. Over and out."

I watch him put his hand on the doorknob. He tips his head back, giving me one last glare, and then he's gone.

For good this time.

I feel empty, like a perfume bottle without any spritz left, just the lingering scent of what used to be inside. And no matter how pretty the bottle, how ornate the glass, nothing else can come out. Not a drop.

I squeeze my pillow and hurl it across the room. Mom would kill me if she saw me. She paid out the nose for these squishy squares of cloth, but I don't care. I don't care about anything.

I sit in silence, aching from my chest to my eye sockets down to the spaces in between my toes. I shiver and rub my hands up and down my arms.

I heave out of the folds of the couch to get a sweatshirt. I find Tia's pink hoodie on a hook in the laundry room and grab a handful of tissues to mop my face. My purse is propped against the Kleenex box. Grabbing my phone, I group text my roomies.

Keegan stopped by. Total blow out. Feel like a flat tire.

Zhooopp.

After sending the message, I squeeze my eyes and stomp my foot.

Kat's brother is in the ER, and I'm whining about my boyfriend! Lovely. Why don't I think before I speak, or text? I turn off my phone so I can't even see the sweet responses they'll most likely send as a punishment for me being so selfish. Why am I so selfish?

Sliding my phone back in my purse, I bump my journal.

Snatching the cloth-covered book, I dash upstairs. I need to get all this down in my journal, but the words won't flow if I'm goopy and unsettled. I slide out of my outfit and into soft yoga pants and a long-sleeve cotton tee. I pull Tia's sweatshirt over my head. In the bathroom I use warm water to remove all the tears, mascara, makeup, and mayhem from my face. I want to get my words down while it's still quiet, before Mom comes back with Tia.

I sigh, sinking into my bed, wiggling into the perfect spot. My king-size mattress is like a spa compared to my bunk in the dorm. I pull my comforter around me, prop my biggest pillow behind my back, and settle in with a pen.

When was the last time I was completely by myself? There's always someone in our dorm room. Even at night, when we're all asleep, Hannah talks in her sleep, ensuring there's never silence. And when I'm not there, I'm dashing off to class or the dining hall or a meeting for the *QuadAngles*, our school magazine.

I listen hard to the silence. There's a pleasant hum from the heater, but that's it. Peaceful. Quiet. Okay. Maybe now I can think.

The binding on my journal cracks pleasantly as I open the pages.

FALL BREAK

I write in thick, dark letters with my favorite felt tip pen, loving their permanence. My thoughts, ideas, beliefs, resolutions, memories are all so much more real, more solid, when I see them in ink.

Off to a banner start. I had dreams of relaxing family time, curled by the fireplace laughing and telling stories. I wanted to escape the stress of school in the sanctuary of home.

But then—BAM—we get to Kat's house and her brother's been in a horrible accident, and we're off to the hospital. Poor Kat. ☹

At home, Mom tells me I'm fat. Thanks, Mom, good to see you too.

Then Keegan comes over. I knew I had to see him over break, but it was supposed to be tomorrow when I was ready. Instead, I was freaked out and vulnerable, so I let my guard down and completely made out with Keegan, which was not the plan, and confused e-v-e-r-y-t-h-i-n-g. Then he broke up with me. It was supposed to be the other way around—me breaking up with him, triumphant. Not him breaking up with me, deflated.

Maybe Mom's right. Maybe Keegan isn't "the one." Hannah said earlier in the semester, "Maybe there's someone that's even better for you than Keegan."

I stare at the prom picture sitting on my dresser. I loved that dress, the perfect lilac color to compliment my Italian complexion. Keegan even got a matching bow tie. We look so happy—so head-over-heels. These days he seems less and less like Prince Charming and more like a villain.

What happened? Was it college? I haven't been gone that long. And I haven't changed . . . that much. I retrace the roller coaster of our recent fights and kiss and makeups.

Thunder jumps onto my bed, making a heavy vibrating sound from the back of her throat. I pet her head. Her purring gets louder, and I aimlessly move my fingers behind her ears as she arches her head in delight.

"Was it college that did this, Thunderkinz?" I ask.

She shakes her head back and forth, like she's shaking off a flea, then starts the stepping up and down ritual she always performs before settling in.

"You're right. It's not school. It happened before I left." I gnaw on the plastic end of my pen.

Sex, I write.

He wants it. I don't. He feels slighted. I feel . . . What?

I feel squeezed, squished so tightly I can barely breathe. When Keegan touches me, I want him to touch me more. It's like I'm in a dream, only aware of him and me. Maybe I should start wearing armor. I have to battle myself and him to keep from going too far.

What if God has someone else planned for me? My pen writes the words and outlines them with a curvy cloud.

Who, God? I wonder.

Does it matter?

Yes! Yes, it matters! Who is it? That cute guy, Michael, on the magazine staff? He seems to really have his act together, but he might be a little arrogant. I answer the question floating through my heart.

Nothing.

It drives me crazy when God doesn't answer me. It drives me even crazier knowing He only does that when I ask things He doesn't need me to know.

Does it matter who it is? Maybe not.

The silence is warm and almost curvy, like God's telling me, "Duh, that's what I just said."

I pick up my pen again. *If I know it's not Keegan, but I trust there is someone else, can I move forward?*

Good question. How do I go from here? I roll back my shoulders and lengthen my spine. Of course I can go from here. I just need to figure out how.

"Palm-er!" Tia squeals, bouncing into my room. Thunder opens one eye in time to see the junior version of me, long dark hair, brown cat eyes, olive skin, and the straight white teeth Mom and Dad forked over a small fortune for at the orthodontist, plop onto my bed.

CHAPTER ELEVEN – CLAIRE

"MOVING?" A PIECE OF BOK Choy, sharp with garlic and ginger, sticks in my throat. "Where?"

"Not from Cleveland." Mom looks away and inserts the tabs in all of the little white cardboard boxes. "Just across town."

"Where across town? When?" I take a huge bite of crunchy egg roll.

"Well, you know . . ." Mom's voice quivers as she clears the boxes. "We lived here because it was between your high school and mine. We could both catch buses from the stop on the corner, and it worked. But, well . . ." She exhales, her voice all twitchy,

"You're not here anymore." Mom opens the fridge.

"I've been gone for eight weeks, and I'm NOT done eating yet." I stand up and take boxes of rice and sweet and sour shrimp from the counter and carry them back to the table, protecting my food so she can't take it away like she's taking away my home. I am so hungry and so empty and so not in control.

"Oh." Mom looks at me, then at the fridge, then back to me. She wrinkles her nose, like she always does right before she cries. It trembles. "Sorry. I guess I've just been eating by myself . . ."

My cheeks flush warm. I didn't mean to make Mom cry. Nothing is going the way I thought this visit would.

"It's all right." I kiss her cheek and sit back down. "Sorry you have to eat alone. That's kinda sad."

Mom sniffs. "I've just gotten into my own routine. I bet you have too. I've been doing yoga almost every night at the Y, and by the time I come home, I just eat something while grading papers and settle into a show or a book before bed. I haven't eaten at the table in . . ." She shrugs. "I don't know when." The fridge clicks shut, but Mom continues to hold the door handle.

"Is your new place near Susan and Trent's?" I ask, hoping if Mom's closer to her best friend, she won't be as lonely all the time.

"No, but it's close to my school and the Y. It's smaller, a one-bedroom, but it will suit me fine. I can actually walk to work." She comes back to the table with a faint smile.

I twirl a strand of hair around my index finger, but what I want to do is jump out of my seat and shake her. How can she move? This is the only place I've ever lived.

"No more worrying about catching the bus. Can you imagine? Plus, I'll save a bit on rent."

"One bedroom?" I look toward my room. "Where will I sleep? I'll still come home sometimes, Mom. Like *all* summer."

"We'll make it work." Mom clutches the table, like she'll collapse if she doesn't hold on tightly enough. "You can sleep on the couch, or we could share my room. You share a room with three girls at school, for goodness' sake." Mom's voice gets faster and higher. "It's all set. Be happy for me, Claire."

I don't enjoy making Mom upset. Really, I don't. It's just this is how it always goes—how it's always been. Mom acting like a little girl who needs to be coddled, usually when I need her most. I came home looking for a little love and comfort. But instead, Mom's moving, didn't even have the guts to tell me, and now she's the one who's upset. I'm so tired of holding her up, when it's so much work just to hold myself up.

"Why is this such a happy thing? Is this because of the greeter guy at church? Does he live your new neighborhood?" I deliberately pile more rice and shrimp on my plate, more than I'll ever be able to eat.

Mom shrinks. "I don't know where Joe lives. I can walk to work, Claire. Did you hear that part? It's cheaper. It's not all about you. You have college and your roommates and ballet. It's what you always wanted. This is something I want. You can deal with it in the summer." Mom sniffs again and stares at me.

I picture Mom swinging her tote bag down an elm-lined sidewalk to the high school she teaches at in the suburbs—a neighborhood much safer and cleaner than our city block. Less rent is important. I know I'm on scholarship at Clarkston, but there are still expenses, like my bus ticket home. I should be happy for her. She's right. I should be.

Mom's face has gone so white she looks like she's made out of porcelain, like if I say something sharp, she'll shatter. *Say something nice*, I tell myself.

"You'll be happy there." I try to steady my voice. "I can picture you walking down clean sidewalks with no graffiti."

Even if I can see Mom living *there*, I can't get past me not living *here*. All of my memories are here, even back to when Dad was around. And she's right, I do share a room at school, and I love it. Without my roommates I'd unravel. But home was supposed to be an anchor keeping everything in place. A place I don't have to wait in line for the shower behind Palmer or listen to Kat blaring ESPN when I want to nap. A place I can't hear Hannah yapping in her sleep about folding clothes properly. Honest, she does that. In a one-bedroom, where will I go to be by myself—ever? There's not any room in my throat for another bite of shrimp because of the enormous lump.

"When do you move?" My voice feels small.

"Next week."

CHAPTER TWELVE – KAT

I'VE HEARD IF YOU CAN scream out loud in a dream, you can end it, you can make it stop. If only I could scream, but no sound escapes my mouth. I twitch. I will myself to make a noise. I scrunch my entire body into a ball and jerk it out full form to find my vocal chords. The slightest whisper escapes my lips, "No!" I scream again and again each time gaining volume. "No, No, NO! **NO!**"

I jump to sitting, clammy with sweat. Okay, it wasn't real. I'm in my bed. I'm awake! It's okay.

Despite my exhaustion, I slide my feet to the floor. I have to shake away my dream—that horrific nightmare. I try to tighten my groggy brain around my thoughts.

Mama and Daddy should be chattering over the sound of their shower as Daddy gets ready to manage his sales reps from his home office and Mama prepares for her morning as a children's speech therapist at her office in town. But I don't hear anything.

Alex is long gone for swim practice and usually leaves most of the lights on, but the house is dark. The aroma of coffee brewing should fill the air, but instead our home smells flat and blank.

Disturbed by the stillness I click on my light. I stretch out my legs, still stiff from the long car ride home from Clarkston. I grab my sweatshirt from the doorknob and wrap it tightly around me as memories of my dream send shivers down my arms. "Okay, Kat, get a hold of yourself. It was a dream, and it's over," I say out loud. I wrestle with my brain, denying the ghoulish images tangled in the cobwebs of my mind.

"Kat?" Mama's voice croaks in the stillness, making me jump nearly out of my skin.

"Hey, Mama." I mean to ask her why she isn't dressed, why Alex didn't turn the lights on, why the coffee isn't brewing, but Mama's arms encircle my body before I can speak. She hums a familiar song to herself, but I can't place it. She sways us back and forth.

Daddy's one footstep behind her. "Jennifer?" He whispers Mama's name and wraps his arms around both of us.

And here we sit on my bed, Mama, Daddy, and I, staring, swaying. Why does everyone seem so freaked out, including me?

"What's goin' on? Where's Alex?" I blurt.

Mama lets out a sob. Daddy squeezes tighter.

"C'mon, Kat." Daddy tilts his head.

I pry Mama's arms off me. She's still humming and rocking like she didn't hear me. I turn to Daddy.

His voice is a mere whisper. "Remember, sugar, the accident, the police, the hospital."

My throat tightens and a thousand white-hot needles poke my skin. Daddy's jaw clenches. He grabs my hand and pulls Mama and me back tight against him. Then a sound escapes my father's body that I've never heard before. It sounds like a walrus bellowing. I can tell it's coming from him, because his entire body vibrates.

"No!" I shout. "I don't believe you! I wanna see him! No! No! No!" My soul, hot and fiery, feels like it's being yanked from my body, burning my insides as it goes.

Once it escapes my skin, I am left empty, and cold—so completely cold.

Then like a mammoth wave smacks an unprepared surfer, all of the scenes from last night pour over and around me. They encase me in a shocking cold, dark blue umbrella, blurring the world outside the wave.

It was real.

The flashing lights.

The burly policeman.

The tight expression and stubby nails of the surgeon.

The string unwinding from Alex's fist.

Alex didn't go swimming this morning. He wasn't here to wake up and put on his suit and drive to the pool. His car isn't in the garage because it's totaled. The kitchen lights aren't on because he isn't here to turn them on. Our family can wait here forever, but Alex will not come through the door. This is all there is—Mama, Daddy, and me—even though there's a gaping hole only Alex can fill.

"No!" I wail again and collapse face-first into my covers.

"Hmm, hmm," Mama keeps humming.

Alex should be cracking a joke and slapping Daddy on the back and singing a line of that song with Mama, 'cause I know he knows the words. He should be asking us why we're all sitting around and why we don't fry up some eggs or fix a mess of pancakes because he's always hungry. He should be flipping on the TV and turning to ESPN to get the highlights from last night's games.

He should be laughing.

He should be here.

CHAPTER THIRTEEN—HANNAH

MOM PARKS THE CAR. COUNTLESS kids in bright polyester costumes swarm the parking lot, weaving and dodging around bales of hay and piles of pumpkins.

"Yay! Pony rides!" Owen squeals from under his Viking horns.

"And face painting!" Sammie cheers. "What do you think I should get, Hannah?" A heart on my cheek? A flower? No, no, no, a peace sign! You have to get one too, so we can be twins. Please?"

"Are you kidding? I'm all in. I love face painting." I grin, thankful for something, anything to delay having to actually go inside the senior center. "Where did all these kids come from?" I ask Mom. "It looks like a Playhouse Disney convention."

"I guess it's a really big deal." Mom fiddles with a stray hair in the rearview mirror. "It's such a thrill for the seniors. It will be," she pauses, "nice."

Nice is Mom's word for anything tolerable.

"How did Grampa get here from the nursing home? Oh my gosh, were we supposed to pick him up?" I grab Mom's hand.

"Less drama, Hannah." Mom pops her keys into her purse. "Remember, I already told you. They have a shuttle that takes the nursing home residents over here several times a week for events. They brought them over earlier."

Sammie pulls me toward the face-painting table. I'm less anxious and sing quietly, "This is Halloween," feeling slightly festive as a volunteer tickles my cheek with a paintbrush. Sammie and I get matching peace signs, and Owen gets a lightning bolt streaking up his arm.

It's a relief to act like a kid and not worry about what everyone's wearing and how my hair looks and getting to my next class on time. It's an even bigger relief to give my brain a distraction from the thoughts about what happened to Kat's brother. I've called her, but she won't answer her phone. I can't stop thinking about her. But this sensory overload just might help.

Inside we're bombarded by a giant bake sale, someone selling raffle tickets, and dogs in full Halloween regalia.

"We should have so dressed up Ziggy!" I squeal, patting a terrier wearing a Spider-Man suit. "He could have been a vampire."

"Or one of the guys from One Direction!" Sammie squeals.

"How would we do that?" I look at her and laugh.

I buy a plate of cupcakes sprinkled with candy corn as Mom checks in at the front desk to see where Grampa is in this melee.

She motions for us. I lick sweet chocolate frosting off the edge of my cupcake and get Sammie and Owen to follow her. "Delish!" I proclaim, taking the rear. Seniors propped in chairs and wheelchairs line the hallway.

Crossing the boundary of the lobby to the hallway my jaw locks. The abrasive smell of rubbing alcohol and bleach is not enough to overpower the lingering scent of urine. Sammie and Owen hold out their trick-or-treat bags as elderly folks fill them with Tootsie Rolls, Nerds, and Dum Dums. I toss the rest of my cupcake in the nearest trash can.

One man has stringy pieces of gray hair sticking out from under an orange yarn Raggedy Ann wig. Did he pick that wig to be funny, or is he so mentally out of it he doesn't know what he's doing? I shift my eyes so I won't stare. I really don't want to stare. I hate myself for almost staring and also for not being able to look him in the eyes.

A woman wears brown furry puppy dog ears attached to a headband on top of her silver head. Another sports a paper mask of a duck pushed way up to her forehead, probably because it's so hard to see out of the tiny eyehole slits. Most of the seniors have someone next to them, a relative or a nurse, helping them pass out candy. Are they happy? Does the excitement of children in costumes bring them joy? Do they all know what's going on? Do the noise and shuffling and masks and makeup confuse them?

"What are you?" a bald man asks Sammie.

"A witch." She spins in a circle, her cobweb cape billowing around her black leggings and turtleneck. The sparkly peace symbol on her cheek matches the sequins on her pointy hat, the glitter makeup I applied around her eyes, and the glimmering threads woven into her cape.

"What are you?" she asks the man as he stuffs a Snickers in her sack.

"I'm an old man." He smiles.

We laugh and turn the corner into the large common area filled with sofas and televisions and more old people.

"Sammie, don't you look adorable!" Grampa's voice breaks through the choruses of "trick or treat."

"And, Owen. You nearly scared me right out of my pants!"

"*Grr!*" Owen contorts his face into a wicked grin.

"Yikes!" Grampa fake jerks back in his wheelchair. He looks like someone shrunk him and put him in an extra-large sweater.

"Hi, Grampa," I say, focusing on his twinkling blue eyes. They still look the same.

"Hannah Banana." He smiles, reaching out to me from his wheelchair. "What a treat. How's school?"

I lean forward so I can hug him, but he feels fragile under his burgundy cabled cardigan.

"It's good. I love college. It's good to see you." I keep my eyes honed into the cool calmness of Grampa's eyes, not wanting to see the wheelchair, not wanting to acknowledge it. His eyes seem happy.

"Quite an event you have going on here," Mom says, taking the handles of his chair and wheeling him into a space away from the chaos.

"The kids all look so darn cute." He shakes his head and exhales—a little too much like a gasp for air. "Sit down. Sit down." He motions.

Sammie and Owen plop down in a couple of chairs, sorting through their candy. Mom sits on the edge of a pastel blue sofa that looks like it was recovered in 1984 and tilts her head toward me, indicating a spot next to her.

"Okay," I whisper.

I don't want to sit on this sofa. Is it clean? What if someone's Depends leaked? What if a hundred someone's Depends leaked? I pop a piece of cinnamon gum into my mouth attempting to chew the thought away.

"Now, why didn't you wear a costume, sweetheart?" Grampa asks.

"I think I'm getting too old for all of that, don't ya think?"

"Hopefully not too old to do a crossword with your grampa?" He winks.

"Never ever too old for that."

He shuffles through a pile of newspapers and magazines in a pouch on the side of his wheelchair. He finds the newspaper and his glasses and slides them on his nose.

"Do you have a pen, Polly?" he asks Mom.

"Sure, Dad." She pulls one from her purse and elbows me toward Grampa. "Tell Grampa all about college, Hannah. He keeps asking me how you're doing, but you'll have to give him the real story."

"Ah, yes, college." He opens the newspaper to the puzzle and folds back the page. "How are your grades?"

"They're good, Grampa." I nod and try to think what would interest him. "I'm taking a Botany class, which is pretty boring, but there's a very cute boy in it." I smile. "My English prof is awesome. He speaks in a real British accent," I say in my best Hermione Granger voice. "And my Theories of Learning class is so cool. I can tell I'm going to love my major."

"What exactly is your major?" Grampa takes the cap off the pen.

"Elementary Ed. I'll be certified to teach K–5."

For the next hour Grampa and I discuss college life, Sammie and Owen plow through six or seven pieces of candy each, and Mom goes back and forth between monitoring their bickering and guiding the conversation. I can tell she's trying to make sure we entertain Grampa. She looks tired and heavier than I remember. Good thing I tossed that cupcake. If I have her chubby genes, which I'm pretty sure I do, I'll have to keep taking spinning and avoid Halloween candy.

"Eight letter word for 'hungry'?" Grampa asks.

"Ravenous," he answers himself before I can even open my mouth.

I glance at the clock. It's mounted between two crudely painted landscapes of the beach. I hope a senior citizen painted them, otherwise, they have the worst decorator in the history of the world. How long are we supposed to stay?

"Three letter word for 'Indian tribe,'" he reads.

"Ute," we say in unison.

"What's an oot?" Owen asks.

"Some kind of Indian that always fits in our crossword puzzles. We think because of the vowels." I shrug.

"Oot-a-loot-loot. Fancy-wancy suit." Owen taps his legs in a drumming rhythm.

"Oota moot fruit, we sure got alotta loot," Sammie chimes in.

"Hoot, hoot, hoot, said the owl wearing boots," I add, laughing.

Grampa tosses his head back, the corners of his eyes crinkle. "Oot a root flute da doot da doot doot."

"Looks like you all are having a good time," a large nurse with brown hair pulled back with a zillion clips and a wide smile outlined in cherry red lipstick says. "About five more minutes until they start loading the bus, Mr. Trager."

Grampa winks at her. "Rose, I'd like you to meet my grandkids. This beautiful witch is Sammie. And the fierce Viking is Owen."

Owen growls at the nurse to show off.

"And this young lady, without a costume, is Hannah. She's in college, you know. And you've met my daughter-in-law, Polly. Right?"

"Of course I have, sir. Aren't your costumes wonderful?" Rose's smile makes me forget for a minute how long I've been here. "Did you two get lots of good candy?"

"Lots!" Sammie smiles. "Want a piece?"

Owen just growls again.

"No thanks, dear, but sure is kind of you to offer. What nice manners. And college." She looks at me. "What are you studying?"

"Elementary Ed at Clarkston."

"Very good. That's a great school, Clarkston. You must be smart. Well, nice to meet you all. Let me know if you need anything else, Mr. Trager. You should probably be wrapping up your visit. I'll swing back by in a few to help roll you up the ramp."

I exhale, physically relieved to go—not to leave Grampa, just the purveying scent of mothballs. I wish we could kidnap him and sneak him out with us. He still seems funny, totally in the conversation, normal, well, except for the wheelchair.

"Sure thing, Rose," Grampa says.

As Rose saunters off, Grampa whispers, "I'm pretty sure she likes me."

CHAPTER FOURTEEN – PALMER

"CAN I BORROW YOUR MICHAEL Kors jacket?" Tia asks, batting her eyelashes while I pack.

"As in the one I'm wearing?" I ask. "I did wear it last week at school and over the weekend at home. Maybe I could part with it. Only if I can borrow your fur vest." I wink.

"Deal!" Tia scurries off to her room to fetch her vest. I scamper after her, seeing the potential here.

"What if," I suggest, "I leave my black boots here, and I borrow your brown ones?"

"Until Thanksgiving?" Tia frowns.

"No, just for a couple of days. I'm coming right back Tuesday night for Alex's funeral on Wednesday morning." I swivel my wrists, emphasizing the turning around part. "It doesn't seem real, T. I only met Kat's brother, I think, twice, but he's gone gone, like not coming back gone."

"Creepy." Tia shivers and scrunches her face.

"I know, right?"

"Can you just skip class like that?"

"I e-mailed my profs to let them know I'm missing class on Wednesday. Two of them were cool, the third was a jerk. 'Thank you for alerting me of your absence on Wednesday, Miss Ruscilli.'" I hold pretend glasses up to my eyes and repeat the e-mail in a nasally tone. "'As the syllabus states, class attendance is optional, however your participation grade is dependent on your presence. Any work missed is simply that, missed. Please make your decision accordingly.'"

"You're going to a funeral, for crying out loud!" Tia rolls her eyes.

"So much for The Impact of the Berlin Wall on Modern Culture. At least it's not one of my journalism classes." I wave my hand.

"I'm gonna see if lunch is ready," Tia says, gathering my black boots like a treasure.

"All right."

I slide the silver cross on the chain around my neck from side to side, glancing around my room. Keegan's face catches my eye from our prom picture. I pick it up. He didn't call or text after our fight.

Not once.

It is—we are—completely, truly, and officially over.

I slip the picture into my dresser drawer where it can't stare at me. The stuffed animals Keegan gave me on various holidays and won for me at the State Fair sit piled on the bench in the corner of my room. I gather them in a lump and shove them under my bed.

I exhale.

I don't like them under there, trapped in a dark, dusty place. It's not their snuggly little selves' faults he's a jerk, but I can't stand to look into their sweet, droopy eyes— they're too much like Keegan's sweet, droopy eyes.

I stomp down to the basement in search of a cardboard box.

"Mom made pasta salad," Tia calls from the kitchen.

"Okay," I call back, finding exactly what I need—the giant box Mom's new ottoman arrived in, the cranberry-colored one that her decorator said Mom couldn't live without. "I'm just organizing my room. I'll be ready to eat in a few."

Back upstairs, I pull the stuffed animals back out from under my bed and lay them gently in the bottom of the box. I pile my prom dress, all the flowers Keegan gave me that I'd pressed as keepsakes, and the stack of cards I've saved from our anniversaries, birthdays, graduation, etc., on top. The top card pictures two squirrels smooching on the front. I slide my finger along the side, opening it a crack, longing to read Keegan's words to me, his message of love, to fill the emptiness that slowly swallows me, to remind myself he did love me. That I was loved.

"No!" I scold myself.

Closing the card, I slice my finger along the thin edge. The sting of the paper cut returns my resolve. I'm furious at Keegan. I do not miss him. Right? It's his fault I got this paper cut.

I suck my finger, tasting the metallic tinge of blood. After nursing the sting, I cram the card back in the rubber band, binding the Hallmark memories together, and shove the stack along the side of the giant box. I heap more pictures and frames and CD mixes into the box, concealing my memories from view. If I'm going to move on with things, I'll need a clean slate, a clean room, one that's free of the reminders muddling my brain and heart.

"I almost forgot. Wanna swap scarves?" Tia pokes her head back into my room. "Whatcha doing?"

I freeze with my hand half in, half out of the box.

CHAPTER FIFTEEN – KAT

ALEX'S SALTY DOG CAFÉ T-SHIRT sits on top of my stack of clean laundry. I hold my breath, eyeing it like it's a ghost, then grab the shirt and clutch it to me, confirming it's real. Alex bought it the time we went to Hilton Head for spring break after we'd spent the afternoon eating pizza on the patio and listening to some guy play acoustic guitar. I exchange my shirt for his, pulling it over my head. It's soft and roomy. I walk zombie-like into Alex's room and close the blinds, making it pitch-black, and unplug his clock so the red numbers can't glare at me. I turn off my phone, which vibrates with texts from Hannah and Palmer and Claire. I don't want to read them. I can't bring myself to talk. What would I say? I don't have anything to say to anyone . . . anyone but Alex.

I have a million questions for him, but he's been stolen from me. I've been robbed of my time with him, denied the chance to ask Alex why this happened and did it hurt? And if so, how badly? And does he miss me like I miss him?

Why, God? How could You let this happen? Why did You let this happen?

But I don't wait for God's answer; I don't really want to hear it. Nothing He can say will make sense. Nothing He can say will make it better. I crawl under Alex's covers and pull them over my head, shutting out everything. They smell like Alex, like his shaving cream.

"No electric razor for me," Alex announced when the hair on his lip grew in. "If I'm gonna shave, then I'm gonna shave like a man. I'm gonna lather up all white like Santa and slide a real razor across my face. That's shavin'!"

I close my eyes, inhaling the fresh, clean fragrance of Edge. I picture Alex strutting around the bathroom, singing into his razor like a microphone. I close my burning eyes, snuggle into his cool navy blue sheets, and pull the covers close to my chin. I allow myself to succumb to the absolute darkness, melting into the sheets.

Sometime later I hear someone knocking, and maybe even the door opening, but I don't have the energy to answer. I roll over and fall back into my abyss.

It's my bladder that eventually pulls me back into consciousness. Emerging from my dream state, my eyes adjust to the dark. I'm not in my bed. I'm in Alex's. There's only one reason I'm here, and that's because he's not.

From half-slumber, tears stream down my face, hot and tired and painful. I reach out, lift the blinds, and peek out the window. *Remember all the times you kicked the ball with me out there, Alex? All the times we raced to the mailbox?*

Outside is gray. Is it dusk or dawn or is it fixin' to rain? Does it matter? I don't want to move, but I need to pee. Really badly. I stretch and shuffle down the hall. My stomach growls. When did I last eat? What time is it now? I'm famished. A bathroom stop, a quick bite of food, and then I'll crawl back in bed.

Climbing down the stairs I'm bombarded by Mama's shrieks.

"Why? He had everything! He had his whole life in front of him! Why him?" Her voice is all wrong, like it was transferred onto a balloon that is being blown up and stretched until it's so distorted it's just a disturbing image of what Mama's voice used to be.

I peer into the kitchen and see Daddy with her. I stand there, watching them. I inch close enough I could reach out and touch them, but I'm not sure if I'm solid, if I'm actually in the kitchen or if I'm watching my parents from far away.

"Kat." Daddy's voice confirms I'm real. They're real.

"Hey," I squeak, shuffling away from my folks and over to the cupboard where I pull out the peanut butter.

"Oh, good, darlin'." Mama closes her eyes tightly, as if it will erase what she just said. Does she think I didn't hear her? That she can make it go away? She lifts her head slowly. When she speaks again her voice is raspy, distant. "You need to eat."

"I know." I slide open the silverware drawer and pull out a knife. It clanks unusually loudly. Or is everything else unusually quiet? I grab a loaf of bread and undo the twist tie, releasing the fresh bakery smell. I spread the peanut butter in silence. My folks don't say a word, but I feel their eyes on me, and I'm pretty sure it's not because they want to watch me make a sandwich. I grab a banana from the fruit basket and slice thin, even circles onto the brown goo spread across my bread. I don't want what they said to penetrate my brain. I don't want anyone to say anything else. Maybe if I just go through ordinary motions, everyday movements, they'll forget I'm here, and I can slip back up to Alex's room.

Slice, slice, slice.

"Come on and sit down, sugar." Daddy motions toward the table.

Four chairs. Three of us. There might as well be a neon sign attached to the empty seat flashing the message, "**Alex's empty chair**!"

I take a bite of the sweet, gooey sandwich.

"We were talkin' about—" Mama scrunches a tissue in the palm of her hand.

"I know it's painful, sugar, but we're just tryin' to make sense of this mess." Daddy takes over Mama's sentence.

I take another bite. "How can we make sense of it? It's not fair. How could God let this happen?"

Mama and Daddy stare at me like I'm the devil himself.

"There, I said it. We're all thinking it. Why would God let this happen?" I grab Mama's hands, but she pulls away. I look to Daddy.

"I don't know." Daddy shakes his head.

Why, God? Why did You let this happen? Why?

The words bang against each other in my head as I take another bite. The banana's sweet and perfect with the salty peanut butter. The bread is soft and fresh.

"It could be foul play." All of a sudden Mama's eyes get this wild look. "Or a conspiracy."

A conspiracy? I turn away from Mama's psycho rant, not even acknowledging it, and methodically chomp on my sandwich, bite, chew, chew, bite, chew, chew.

Mama gets up and paces back and forth across the kitchen. Her shoulders are so tense they look like they might snap off. Her slippers make a shuffling sound across the hardwood floors. Daddy wipes his face with a giant white handkerchief. His jaw is clenched so tight it reminds me of the skeleton in Biology that had wires holding its jawbone shut.

Alex hugged me good-bye when he dropped me off at Clarkston. That was the last time I touched him. Since then it's been a zillion texts and FaceTime, but those were all funny and teasing and silly. I didn't tell him what an awesome brother he was, or how much I loved him, like, crazy loved him.

What if I'd said more? Could I have gotten one more of his bear hugs, one more piece of brotherly advice? The uneasiness spreads from my core, starting at my heart and pushing out toward my lungs, making it hard to breathe. The pressure punches my stomach, punch after punch. It presses up toward my throat, searching for an escape route. My stomach feels like a jar of peanut butter, brown and gooey and roasted. It lurches inside me, and I run for the sink. One big violent surge and everything I've ever eaten is going down the drain. I will the images of Alex, unconscious and pale, down the drain with my sandwich.

CHAPTER SIXTEEN – CLAIRE

I CLOSE THE LID OF the giant cardboard box. As I unroll the packing tape it squeaks and squeals, seemingly shrieking at me, "You're never coming back!"

"Maybe I don't want to come back," I tell the box quietly enough that Mom can't hear.

Mom and I keep our combined wardrobe in her room. The closet in my bedroom is so rinky-dink, we use it to stash paperwork—Mom's taxes, warranties and manuals, copies of the divorce proceedings, proof that Dad is supposed to be paying child support. If he ever resurfaces, Mom could wave one of those papers in his face.

Besides clothes, I don't have a lot of other stuff, but what I have—the ceramic ballet shoes I painted at a pottery birthday party, the posters I'd stuck to my walls of European cities and ballerinas in flight, the books I devour to escape reality, even the covers and sheets from my bed—all in this box. Crazy my whole life can fit in a box . . . one box.

I stick out my tongue at the tape.

Is it possible to pack a past? There's not a lot from my past I want to bring with me. Clarkston was the new start I'd longed for. Maybe Mom moving away from the memories of Dad, away from the memories of our struggles, away from the memories of her deep, depressed funks will force us both to move on. Maybe I can pack the memories of the rape, the damage it's done to me, and seal it with squealing, sticky tape.

"I think that's it, Mom." I walk out of my room.

"Oh."

My eyes bulge at the emptiness of the family room. While I've been packing my room, Mom's taken down our framed prints, leaving the walls stark except for the old water stains the pictures hid. The rug is rolled up in a corner next to the pictures, exposing deep scrapes and gouges on the floor. All that's left is the couch, the TV, and a small table. Even the magazines and coasters from the coffee table and the DVDs stacked next to the TV have disappeared. Vanished.

This doesn't look like our apartment. It looks like anyone's apartment, or no one's apartment. All the traces of Mom and Claire have been erased.

"I figure all I need this week is a place to sit and grade papers and maybe watch some TV to unwind." Mom shrugs. "I think I'll be in pretty good shape when Susan helps me pack the U-Haul next weekend."

"Right." I twist my ponytail into a bun and tuck the end under the rubber band.

"I'll take some of the things over in carloads this week. The manager at the new place said I could store some boxes there before my official move-in date on Saturday."

I picture Mom's friend and her husband each carrying one end of the couch out the door with Mom riding on top.

"I've lived here my entire life," I say.

"I've lived here longer. Your dad and I moved in two years before you were born. Twenty years." Mom wraps a coffee mug in newspaper. "Twenty years of clangy pipes and flights of stairs. Did I tell you my new place has an elevator?"

"No."

How many times have I climbed those stairs or rolled back to sleep in the middle of the night to the familiar clang of pipes?

"When I come back for Thanksgiving, it won't be to here." I curl into a corner of the couch, trying to permanently scan the room into my brain.

"Oh, I was going to tell you." Mom tears off a piece of the classifieds, the rip sharp and poignant, as if to announce something big. "We're going to Denise's for Thanksgiving this year. We'll take the bus to Detroit that Wednesday after school and stay the whole weekend. Won't that be fun?"

Denise is Mom's older sister, and even though she's my only aunt, I would never call her my favorite aunt. "Why are you so quiet, Claire?" Denise asks every meal I've ever eaten with her. "Boys like chatty girls. Girls like chatty girls. No wonder you don't have very many friends."

That's her grand advice.

"How would *I* get there?" I ask Mom, unwrapping my bun and running my fingers through my hair, loosening it against my shoulders.

"Oh dear." Mom sighs. "I hadn't thought of that. I've been so absorbed with the move."

You've been absorbed with your dramas the entire eighteen years I've lived in this apartment, I think to myself, smart enough to know those comments just make Mom shrivel and dissolve, and therefore aren't worth saying out loud. Not now. Not ever, really.

"Maybe you could take the Greyhound from Clarkston to Detroit?"

How unpleasant would that be? Taking the bus into downtown Detroit to spend three days with Aunt Denise telling me not to be shy.

"Maybe."

CHAPTER SEVENTEEN – KAT

I PLUG MY PHONE INTO Alex's computer to sync his songs off iTunes. It immediately vibrates with unchecked messages, voice mails, and texts. I'm so not up for all that.

I growl at my phone, signaling it to stop. Right on cue, a new text zips across the face of my phone from Nicholas. Nicholas was Alex's best friend. He also happens to be one of the two boys I recently kissed at school. The other one is Tony, but I don't have space in my muddled mind to think of him right now.

Are you ok? I keep calling & no one answers. I've left you a million messages. I understand if you want to be alone. I just need to know you're all right. I loved Alex too.

I twirl the silver thumb ring on my left hand.

I'm here. Some times better than others. Nothing makes sense. I know you and Al were tight. He thought of you as a brother.

There. That should ease Nicholas's conscience some and maybe clear me from answering the messages on my phone from him.

Zzzup.

Uh, no, Nicholas. We aren't playing textersation here.

Wanna talk? Hang out? I'm here for you.

No. I don't. I don't want to see anyone. Ever.

The hinges of my jaw twinge. My eyes fill again, not pouring down tears for once, but warm in the edges, and not because of Alex this time, but because Nicholas is so genuinely kind to me.

My lime green thumbnail hovers over my phone, then I set it down. I scan Alex's playlist to avoid having to answer Nicholas right away. All our favorites are here, plus lots of his songs. Taylor Swift? Seriously, Alex? But it's not Taylor's poppy boppy "never ever" rant. Instead, her voice is hauntingly entwined with the harmonies of The Civil Wars.

"You'll be all right. No one can hurt you now," she sings.

I feel a harsh whispery sound in the back of my throat. I inhale to try to stop it, but I don't have the strength. A sob explodes from my core.

I pray Alex is all right. That he can't hurt anymore. But what about me? Imagining Alex alone in his crushed car falling from the sky, I bury my head in my arms on his desk, hiding my tears even though there's no one to see them. I hate it when I cry. It makes me feel weak, and I hate feeling weak, so then I get angry with myself. And then I'm sad and mad and worn out. But I can't stop, can't get back to normal. My ribcage aches.

The last text buzzes again, because I never did anything with it.

Alex adored Nicholas. But he never met Tony, the soccer stud who sends a zing through me every time we chat. It seems like I met Tony in another life. Right now I need something, anything, someone.

Sure. C'mon over, but I'm warning you, I'm a mess

I'll be there in 5

Before I can throw all my Kleenex away, the doorbell rings. I don't know where Mama or Daddy are, so I head down stairs and open the door.

Nicholas, all redheaded and freckly, stands there in jeans and an untucked yellow tee with a plaid shirt unbuttoned over it, like a jacket. Sperrys on his feet are the final touch making him look like he stepped out of a J.Crew catalog. I swear he did not dress like this in high school.

"You wanna go for a walk," he asks, tilting his head to the world outside my house.

The wind whispers through tree branches, knocking loose leaves of golden yellow and bright scarlet into the air. They float in spirals to the ground.

I'd assumed he'd come in and we'd hang out in the family room, like he and Alex and I always did. I haven't left the house since . . . since we got back from the hospital. I kinda forgot that was an option.

I tip my head out the door frame. The crisp autumn day hits me in the face, soothing the sting in my eyes.

"Yeah. Let me grab some shoes."

"You might want a jacket too," Nicholas calls as I run back in the house.

A minute later I'm back at the door where Nicholas politely waits on our welcome mat, hands behind his back. I can't wait to get out, to escape.

I step onto the porch, like it's a whole other world.

"I brought you a chai." Nicholas pulls a paper cup with a plastic lid from behind his back.

The sweet, spicy scent wafts my way. It's the first lovely thing I can remember in days. I reach for the cup.

"Thanks." I smile, holding the warmth in my hands, letting it seep into my skin. I bow my head, eyes closed, over the cup and let the herbal aroma tickle my nose. This warmth and this smell surround me.

"You look like you're praying to the tea." Nicholas laughs lightly, like a leprechaun.

I think about that before answering. "I almost am, I guess." I shrug. "I haven't felt or smelled anything so nice since, well . . . since . . ."

"Taste it," Nicholas says.

"Mmm." I savor the flavor rippling across my taste buds. "This must be what heaven's like."

"It'll be even better." Nicholas's eyes twinkle. He slides his arm around me gently as we walk. "God just gives us hints of how amazing heaven will be, and chai's your hint."

"You really think Alex is smellin' cloves and feelin' warm and cozy with a sweet taste on his tongue?" I tap my thumb ring on the lid.

"Something like that." Nicholas laughs again, but not at me, more for me, like a gift, to bring me happiness.

"Heaven? Like chai tea? I think you're crazy sometimes, Nick."

"Maybe." Nicholas smiles and we walk, taking the smallest sips from our cups and contemplating the beauty of a brewed beverage. Nicholas has never been one to push a conversation. I'm grateful for his silence.

Fallen leaves crinkle beneath our feet.

"I haven't talked to anyone," I confess. "I haven't said anything to anyone about Alex actually being *dead*," I push the word out, "unless you count the awful conversations with my parents, where all of us want answers and none of us even knows where to start."

"I know." Nicholas squeezes my waist slightly, not too tight to walk, just enough to say he's here, he's listening. "Thanks for letting me come over. I really wanted to see you before I headed back to school." He pauses and lowers his voice. "How soon after the funeral are you coming back? Soon, Kat?"

"I don't think I can," my voice cracks. "I can't see anyone. I can't hold a normal conversation. I can barely stand." I shake my head.

"You're doing it." He smiles. "You're seeing me. You're talking to me. You don't have to stand alone."

CHAPTER EIGHTEEN – PALMER

"I AM SO BAD AT funerals." Hannah turns down the music as she pulls into a parking spot.

I check myself in the mirror one last time, scrape a smudge of lipstick from the inside corner of my mouth, and use my pinky nail to clear any eyeliner or mascara that might have migrated into the corners of my eyes. "There." I smile at myself, closing the visor with a *thunk*.

"No one's good at funerals, are they?" Claire asks, climbing out of the backseat.

Hannah sighs. "Right. But I never know what to say or how to act. Like, should we go shake hands with Kat's dad? Because I don't know him at all, unless you count the day he helped move her stuff into our dorm, but I don't want to seem rude and not say anything. But if I do shake his hand, then what? Saying 'sorry' seems so nothing, like, of course we're sorry, but that doesn't make any of this better."

"We probably couldn't get close to Mr. Wiley in this crowd if we tried." I roll my shoulders back.

"But what if we do?" Hannah continues. "Or Mrs. Wiley? Should we hug her, or is that weird? I stink at this."

"You?" Claire asks, shutting the car door. "You always know what to say. You're good at everything."

"Hardly," Hannah squeaks. It might be the wind, but I think her cheeks turn a little pink.

"I don't like funerals either, but it was a great excuse to buy a new dress." I smooth out the black fabric, trying to convince myself my shopping trip soothed my unsettled heart, even though it didn't.

"Palm . . ." Hannah scolds me with her eyes.

I look down, not able to take her disapproval, not now. Not able to admit we're dealing with things bigger than we know how to handle.

"It is gorge." Hannah's voice softens and she touches my skirt. She must have seen my composure slip. Because she's known me so long, Hannah sees all my layers, even the ones I think I'm hiding.

"Oh, thanks." I over-smile to recover. "And Claire's right." I air-kiss Hannah. "You do come across as perfect, Han. Admit it. It's part of your persona."

"I try." Hannah grins, hugging herself as a cold gust blows right through us.

"But, Claire Bear"—I slide my arm around her waif-like waist, a little envious of how tiny she is—"nobody's perfect at everything. We all have flaws. Some are just more obvious than others."

Claire leans into me, her corkscrew curls tickling my arm.

At the door of the church a life-size picture of Alex is propped on an easel bordered with enormous white magnolias oozing thick perfume. His green eyes pierce the air, just like Kat's do. His shock of whitish-blond hair frames his face like a halo.

I'm halted by his image. My fingers reach toward his face. They trace the outline of Alex's cheek. I'm surprised the surface is smooth, only a picture. He looks so alive. I didn't expect to get so emotional. I barely knew him. But it's more than that. Something tugs deep inside. How can something be so vivid and real one moment, and then be flat and only a memory the next?

Claire's arm, wrapped in mine, tugs me toward the entrance. Her large blue eyes plead with me to come with her, or maybe she's trying to comfort the thing she senses troubles me. The end of Alex? The end of Keegan? The end of how things used to be?

My fingers flutter across the image of Alex, and I allow Claire to pull me into step behind Hannah, who leads the way. The air in the church feels heavy, thick with the fragrance of lilies and mums, startling, almost smothering, after the brisk air outside. It sounds heavy in here too, with plodding music bellowing from the organ, muffled voices, and sniffles from mourners. The rows are jammed, and people linger in the corners and crowd themselves against the walls.

"Where are we going to sit?" Claire asks.

"I thought we were early," Hannah whispers, grabbing her phone and checking the time. "I knew it. We are early, and there's still nowhere to sit. I told you I'm bad at funerals. I didn't even know how early to be," she hisses, more at herself than at us.

"Don't worry," I mumble, walking slowly across the carpet, scanning pews for a place we'll all fit. "Someone will make room for us."

"I don't even know this many people," Claire says.

"Here." Hannah yanks Claire, who's still attached to me, quickly to the left, so we all kind of stumble into a dark wooden pew. We scramble to situate our skirts and purses and selves without disturbing the adults next to us, who look perturbed we've invaded their space.

Hannah hands programs she picked up on the way in to Claire and me. Thankful for the diversion, something to keep my hands busy, I stare at Alex's name on the front. As I open the stiff, cream paper I feel a tap on my shoulder.

"You always did look good in black." Keegan's mouth presses against my ear.

A warm shock shoots down my ear to my heart. I jump, knocking my purse to the floor, where it lands with a soft thud on the carpet. I thought when he left my house the other day it would be the last time I'd ever see him.

"What are you doing here?" I ask, scrambling to grab the lipstick and quarters that rolled out of my purse.

Keegan sits with a handful of guys from high school, all jocks.

"I didn't know him, not really." His deep, familiar voice dances through my brain. "It's just hard to believe a guy from our town, an athlete like me, is gone, just like that." Keegan snaps his fingers. "It could be any of us. Ya know?" Keegan talks like I didn't tell him all about the accident the other night, like this is the first time we've seen each other in weeks and he's giving *me* the story. Like there's nothing wrong between us. His dark eyebrows twitch above his gray eyes. His face is dangerously close to mine. His fresh rainwater scent surrounds me. "The guys and I all came to pay our respects."

"Yeah." My throat is thick. I feel dizzy, from the church and the crowd and from seeing him. I resist the urge to reach out for his strong hand to steady myself.

"Did you see the font they used on the programs? It's really pretty. Take a look." Hannah tugs my sleeve, breaking my trance. The organ music morphs from one mournful tune to another. I face front as Hannah points to the program.

"Is that . . . ?" I can barely make out Claire's whisper.

I trace with my finger along the program a large *K*.

"Thought so," she breathes.

The slight guilt I felt for using Alex's funeral as an excuse to visit the boutique next to the bagel shop has dissolved. I sit up extra straight in my BCBG silk and inhale deeply. Keegan did notice my dress. He said so. And he deserves to feel remorse over what he's lost. He deserves to see how much I don't need him. That I am perfectly fine with my friends. I am fine without him, aren't I? I link my left arm in Hannah's and my right one in Claire's, forming a chain of strength and support.

I feel Keegan's puppy dog eyes right behind me. I inhale again.

At least I look strong and solid.

CHAPTER NINETEEN – KAT

MAMA, DADDY, AND I WALK together from the side entrance toward the mammoth shiny pipe organ by the altar, but we might as well walk by ourselves. We do not touch. We do not talk. We haven't discussed this at all—what's expected of us and who'll be here and what'll actually take place. These are things we used to discuss. We were the family that had weekly meetings and talked about everything. We were, but all that seems to have changed.

Daddy keeps walking forward, and Mama and I keep following, silently behind, passing. It's as if the entire town is here. Teachers, coaches, family, faces I've seen every day and faces I've never seen before gaze forward. The three of us march across the plush carpet to the beat of the dreary music. We settle into the dark wood seats of the front pew. Mama, Daddy, and I do not look at one another, yet the thought of breaking away, of leaving their presence, is so frightening it freezes me to my seat.

I see Daddy's black suit and Mama's black dress out of my peripheral vision. Another thing none of us discussed—the wearing of black. But this morning I looked in my closet and knew I had to wear black. That's what people wear to funerals. It made everything so final, so real. I could barely pull the dress over my head. I could barely look at myself in the mirror, hating the bleak image staring back at me.

The music fades. The lighting dims. The service starts. The pastor swoops his arms in circles and talks about life and death and eternity. I inhale the thick waxy scent of candles dripping. I examine the intricate patterns of individual flower petals, because to look at all the flowers cluttering the altar, arrangement after arrangement of bright, colorful blooms, is too much, obscene and gaudy. Music fills the room and swallows it whole. I feel like I'm being hypnotized.

And then Daddy stands. I clutch his hand for balance as he exits the pew. He can't leave.

"Don't go," I whisper.

"I'm just going to say a few words." Daddy squeezes my hand.

"Me too." I implore him with my eyes. I never told him I wanted to talk, even though he'd asked. What if it's too late? What if Daddy won't let me now? I need to tell all these people who Alex was.

Daddy bites his lip. The tiniest hint of a smile creeps across his face. He nods and pulls me with him. Mama stays in the pew, staring straight ahead, like she doesn't see us, or like she doesn't want to. Together, Daddy and I approach the lectern. It feels good to hold Daddy's hand, to bridge the gap between us.

"You want to go first, sugar?" he whispers.

"Yes, sir." I nod emphatically. I need to speak now, or all the burdens weighing on my heart will crush me.

I slide behind the pulpit and stare into the faces crowding the church. My aunts and uncles from Nashville are here. Teachers from high school are peppered throughout the crowd along with strangers—how did they know Alex? The swimmers fill several rows on the left side, wearing white shirts and dark suits they reserve for formals and days like today. Sleeves, beards, and glasses of Daddy's sales people peek out from behind the chlorine-bleached heads of the swim team.

My knees wobble. Blood rushes in my head, like the roar of a crowd when our team scores, a deafening cacophony. I stand and stare. I realize again where I am. I waver. Can I explain to these people who and what Alex was? My eyes drift to the right. Hannah, Claire, and Palmer sit together, their arms linked like a fence, to protect me, to hold me up. Hannah nods encouragement. Claire, who usually struggles with eye contact, holds my gaze. Palmer rubs her lips together as if she'll speak for me if I can't do it myself. Then I know . . . I can do this.

"Alex was the best person I ever did meet," I start. My voice comes out muffled and in chunks. I clear my throat.

"He was smart and a beast of a swimmer and made everyone laugh." My voice is louder and stronger now—strong enough to tell Alex what I need to tell him, because this is really for him . . . and for me. "Alex was different from anyone I've ever known. He loved everyone. I don't mean his friends or our family, I mean *everyone*. Alex thought everyone was his friend. And I guess they were." I shrug. "He was oblivious to cliques and clubs and colors and class. He'd get his lunch tray and just sit at any old table where there was an empty seat." I snort. "The rest of us are like homing pigeons trained to eat at our special tables with our closest friends. But Alex ate at a different table every day. He'd walk out of class chattin' it up with kids he barely knew. When we moved to Ohio last year, he'd come home from school and tell me amazingly wild facts about different people every day. I'd barely met anyone. We were the new kids, but that didn't matter to Alex. It never did."

A warm mist spreads over me. I smile.

"And that's how he treated people he didn't know." A lump overtakes my throat, like a fuzzy tennis ball I need to swallow before I can speak.

"But I'm his sister and for me, he is . . . he was always . . ." The tears slide from my eyes to my cheeks. "Always there. So"—I clear my throat and inhale—"I just wanted y'all to know the world was a better place because Alex Wiley lived, and I'm a better person because he lived. And if you knew him, well then, you're a better person too." I inhale all the air I can fit in my lungs and smile through the tears.

Through the blur I see Alex standing by the back door, arms crossed over his chest, grinning.

Daddy moves to the microphone, and I step aside, keeping my eyes glued on Alex. Daddy says a few words and then we sit. I try to pay attention to the other people speaking, the songs being sung. But I can't stop craning my head, trying to see Alex, who is still standing in the back and appears pretty interested in what people are saying about him. I'm too consumed with him to notice anything else.

When the service is over, the pastor directs us to stand. Daddy walks toward the doors on the side of the altar, away from the crowds. I take a step after him, numb, but realize this won't get me to Alex. I spin on my heel and try to head back up the center aisle. By now, everyone else is leaving the sanctuary. Black suits and dark dresses flood the aisles, crowding me out before I make it half way. Bodies block my view, cologne and perfume fill my nose, and music floats from the organ into my ears. Where is he?

"Oh, Kat. I still can't believe it. You okay, sweetie?" Hannah taps my arm and looks at me with puffy eyes. I tilt my head, barely registering my own roommate. I nod and pull away, intent on my mission.

Others touch me and speak, but I am single-minded, oblivious to who they are and what they're saying.

I make my way through the enormous oak doors outside. The crowd is thinner here, but I still don't see him. I rush around the corner, down an alley by a flower shop, then back to the front. I check across the street, but there's no sign of Alex.

"Kat." Someone calls my name, but it's far away and muted through a thousand cotton balls.

"Alex," I plead, my voice cracking, "where are you?"

I stamp my boot, the black ones with fringe that Alex liked so much. "I just need to know where you are!"

"Kat." I feel a hand on my arm and jerk around, thankful to find him at last.

"Nicholas?"

I look past Nicholas's concerned gaze to see if Alex is behind or near him.

"You okay?" Nicholas asks, still holding my arm.

I shake my head, not able to say what I saw or how badly I need to find Alex. I feel weak and empty and collapse in Nicholas's arms.

And it hurts too much. Too much for me to bear. I feel my chest tighten, like it's turning into steel. The part that aches and burns shoves itself deeper into my chest, into the core of my heart. And the steel that's formed around it slams shut, like a locker door. The combination dial whizzes at a dizzying speed, spinning out of control, locking the hurt deep, deep inside.

CHAPTER TWENTY – HANNAH

"WHERE ARE YOU, MATILDA?" THE man propped in his wheelchair screams frantically.

I wonder why one of the nurses doesn't help him. I'm afraid to say something. What if he yells at me? But ignoring him doesn't seem right. Who is this Matilda he's calling for? His wife? His daughter? His dog? I look at his fleshy face and watery eyes, wondering, but his blank expression offers no clues. He clearly misses her, yet one by one people shuffle past him down the hall. Including me.

What if I screamed for help and no one stopped? I chew furiously on my cinnamon gum, hoping it'll help calm me down. I pass a large yellow bag labeled "Biohazardous." I look away, not wanting to process what might be inside. Shots? Blood samples? Okay, brain, don't go there.

Where is Grampa's room?

I can't believe I'm here.

In a nursing home.

By myself.

After attending a funeral.

Plus, I'm skipping class, which makes my blood pressure race fretting about the material I'm missing and if my absence will affect my grade. I could not be more out of my element. But I know I won't see Grampa again until Thanksgiving, and I'm worried about him.

I can do this, right? Please let his room be next. Jesus visited the sick and lame, and even people with leprosy, all the time. *Ew!* How did He do that? I feel pressure in my temples. *Hannah*, I tell myself. *This is the right thing to do.*

Here's Grampa's room. I whistle loudly, hoping if Grampa's not dressed he'll hear me coming and take care of, well, whatever he needs to take care of.

"Hey, Grampa." I paste on my best smile and peek in his room, just a little.

"Hello," Grampa answers, pulling his eyes away from *The Price is Right* flashing on the screen. "They already brought my lunch tray," he says.

I swallow.

"Grampa, it's me, Hannah." I step into the room, where he can see me better, hoping that was the only issue. I walk toward his chair. Thank goodness he's in his chair and not in his bed. Somehow that makes it a little better. I rest my hand on his arm.

"Hannah Banana?" His eyes search me, as if assessing if it's really me. "No one told me you were coming. What a treat."

In his room there is a bed with an army green blanket pulled back. Someone must have helped him out of that bed to sit up for lunch. Two chairs with forest green fabric and pale wooden arms sit stark on the linoleum floor. A mini table on a hinge-like arm, like the desks in some of my classrooms, holds a Styrofoam tray laden with a half-eaten applesauce, a cup of cranberry juice, and something lumpy hiding under suspicious gravy. I glance away. I feel like I'm intruding—his bed, his meal. It's all too personal, oddly intimate and awkwardly exposed.

"I didn't mean to surprise you. I had to come home for a funeral today. Thus the dark outfit." I point to my clothes and launch into a full-speed conversation to cover up my awkwardness. "I had a few minutes before I drive my roommates back to school, and I won't be home again until Thanksgiving, which is only a month away, but still, so I thought I'd stop by and say hi and maybe we could do a crossword?"

"Whose funeral?" Grampa asks. "It wasn't one of the neighbors, was it?"

"No, Grampa. Not one of the neighbors." I pull up a chair and sit next to him. "One of my roommates' brother's, Kat's. He died in a car accident. It was awful."

Grampa's blue eyes clear and seem to register, as if he just woke up. Maybe I did wake him up. I'd nod off I had to watch *The Price is Right*. "That's terrible. Now, remind me, which one is Kat." He sounds more alert now, more like Grampa.

"She's the one who plays soccer." I slide my gum from cheek to cheek. "She transferred to my high school last year. I didn't know her that well, but Palmer had a class with her, and Kat seemed super nice. Then when I saw her at orientation, we all decided to room together."

"Right. Right. So her brother was young, was he?"

"Just a year older than me. Nineteen." It feels good to actually talk about Alex. The accident was a shock. I've been trying to be chipper for Kat's sake, and I was in a whirlwind to get back to school after fall break and turn around and come back for the funeral. I haven't had a chance to get my mind around it.

"Did he have his seat belt on? You know, when I started driving, we didn't even have seat belts. Can you imagine us just bouncing around in our seats?" Grampa's eyes twinkle.

I laugh, picturing Grampa bouncing.

"So you had a little time and you came to see your old grampa. Thanks, Hannah. You're my special girl." He gives my knee a squeeze. "I think the *Times* is over on that counter." He nods toward a pile of papers.

I jut out my jaw, trying to stifle tears. He's my special grampa, but I feel like I'm losing him. He's still so him, but he doesn't fit in this place. Like the "which picture doesn't belong" on Owen's homework worksheets. The one of Grampa in a nursing home. That's which one. I turn my back and recover my composure, finding the *New York Times* and a pen. I turn to the page with the crossword.

Grampa holds out his hands. He always gets to hold the puzzle and the pen. Always. He reads the clues out loud, and we have a contest to see who can answer first, like a game show, but he'd be a way better host than Drew Carey.

"Columbus's ship, five letters," he begins.

"*Pinta*," we say in unison.

Row by row we work our way through most of the across squares.

"Six letter word for 'sailor.'"

"Marine," I answer before him.

"Could be." He rubs his chin. "I'll write it in lightly, just in case."

"We could use a pencil," I tease, already knowing Grampa's answer.

"Pencils are for sissies." He winks. Which is what he says every time he insists on using a pen.

I'm on a roll today, beating Grampa to more words than he beats me. Or maybe he's in a slump. After a long silence, I look over at him.

"You finish for the both of us, will you, Hannah?" he asks, his eyes half-closed.

"But we haven't even started the down clues yet," I protest. This isn't how we do this. We've solved hundreds of puzzles together over the years, and not even when I was little and had no idea what half the words were, or if we were called to the dinner table, or if I was beckoned to bed, did we finish a puzzle without each other. Not once. We might put it down and come back to it after a meal or while the smell of bacon sizzled the next morning, but neither of us ever surrendered.

Grampa opens his mouth to say something but stops.

"Please?" I ask.

"All right then, honey. We'll do the downs in the morning." He exhales loudly and closes his eyes. Just like that. Like someone hit his off button. I stare at my grampa in his chair, chewing my gum, wanting to explain to him I won't be here in the morning.

A soft snore leaks from his mouth.

Do I leave him here alone, sleeping in his chair? Will he freak out if he wakes up and I'm gone? I can't stay. I have to pick up Palmer and Claire, and I need to swing by the house and see Mom too. Should I try to move him to his bed? Should I call a nurse?

I hear crinkling, rustling, crunching and look down to see it's me shaking the newspaper Grampa's placed in my hands.

CHAPTER TWENTY-ONE – KAT

THE ROLLER COASTER CLACKS OVER the broken tracks, faster and faster, closer and closer to the ledge. I open my mouth to scream but no sound comes out. I thunder forward.

Bang. Bang. Bang.

"Kat, you okay in there?"

Daddy's voice and knocks on the door pull me back to reality. I'm tangled in Alex's sheets. There are no tracks. Just his bed. I shiver, soaked with sweat. Is that how Alex felt? Did he feel fear so intense he couldn't even scream? When his car spun out of control, did he will his car to crash to end the nightmare?

I rock back and forth, gasping for air, trying to calm myself.

Inhale. Exhale. Inhale. Exhale.

"Kat?"

"I need a minute, Daddy," I mumble and pull my knees to my chest.

"All right."

I rest my head on my knees, close my eyes, and try to picture something better—Alex never having the chance to be afraid. I imagine him bobbing his head to the tinny guitar riffs of Rascal Flatts, but in my vision a man floats toward Alex's car and lifts my brother to safety. Alex smiles at this man with a kind face, who kind of looks like a hippie with his long hair and beard. Then everything around them is pale and there's no car or wreck, just Alex and this guy and the music. I focus on the stranger's face. His skin is a rich caramel color, and his eyes are liquid like Coca-Cola.

Alex and his rescuer float away from the sickening crunch of metal and the shrill squeal of tires without worrying about walking or running or tripping.

"Kat, sugar, you fell back asleep. Why don't you come on down and get somethin' to eat." Daddy's voice sounds empty, hollowed out. He stands in the doorway.

I stare at him, still trying to orientate myself.

"I ordered Papa John's."

"All right." I brush my rumpled hair out of my eyes. "Just a sec."

Daddy nods and disappears.

The empty hole in my heart stretches as though someone slowly pulls the edges open along one side. *Stretch*—it tears down the other. *Rip*—from the bottom and top at the same time.

I open the blinds and gaze out at the grayness.

My face feels frozen, a stone statue erected in memory of who I used to be. I actually feel my face go from being normal to immobile. I am incapable of crying, or pouting, or smiling, or anything.

An inconceivable sadness rests in my throat, too big for my throat to contain, yet there anyway. It is so thick and so heavy. I might fall forward from its enormity.

I lean my face against the glass of the bedroom window. I could merge with this window, cool, solid, hard, and unmoving. No one would care. Not even my folks. They used to talk to me about everything. We were a family. Now we're just three people living in the same house, like Alex was the only piece of our Jenga tower that kept us from tumbling. Remove him, and we're just a pile of wooden blocks.

After moments, or hours, of standing frozen against the glass, I wonder if I could stay like this for the rest of my life.

The rest of my life? What does that even mean?

CHAPTER TWENTY-TWO – HANNAH

THE SILENCE IS DRIVING ME crazy!

It was actually kind of nice on the drive back from Columbus. I had my headphones on listening to Holly Starr's CD, *Focus*, trying to get myself focused, actually trying to sort out everything in my head—how lonely Grampa must be all the days and hours when no one is visiting him, how many episodes of *The Price is Right* he sits through, how traumatized Kat and her family must be, how I'm going to recover from the classes I missed today. Claire intermittently read and snoozed in the backseat, and Palmer worked on a paper on her laptop. It was easier than talking about what happened, about Alex and Kat.

We're back at our dorm now, holed up in the lounge by the mailboxes, the room with the piano I love. It's become our little study place when our dorm room seems too snug. No one else uses it much. But we're still not saying anything, and my brain is so full it might explode.

I walk over to the smooth, wood bench and slide my hand across the glossy finish before sitting down. Facing the keys, I inhale and gently place my fingers on their solid surface. I don't think about what I'll play. I just start.

And after the opening chords of "Seasons of Love" from *Rent*, I'm singing along softly to the tune. I hear the drumming of someone's pen—I'm guessing Palmer's—

and Claire's whispery voice joining in, "In daylights, in sunsets, in midnights, in cups of coffee, in inches, in miles, in laughter and strife . . ."

"Wow," Claire says when I'm finished. "Hannah, that was so beautiful. Your voice is amazing. When is that audition you were talking about for the a cappella group?"

"It was today."

"What?" Palmer stands and walks over to me. "When?"

"It was this afternoon. I couldn't be at the funeral and the audition." I blow my bangs out of my face, hoping to blow the knot out of my stomach at the same time. "You would have done the same thing."

Palmer looks down, her thick eyelashes fluttering. "I don't know if I would have." She looks back up. "You are the best friend ever, Han."

I'm warmed by Palmer's compliment, the reassurance that I did something right, but I still feel unsteady, second-guessing all of my choices.

"You really skipped your audition for Kat?" Claire peeks at me from where she's curled in the corner of a couch.

I nod. "There's another audition in the spring. I'll try then. I have enough to worry about for now anyway."

"I know, right?" Palmer asks, sitting next to me. "My brain is a mushy mess."

"You too?" I ask. "I keep thinking about Kat, and how wrecked she must be losing her own brother, and then my thoughts drift to what would happen if I lost Sammie or Owen, and I stop. I just can't think about it for another second. So then I start thinking about my grampa, and that's no good either, because I feel selfish because I stopped thinking about Kat. I'm better just playing the piano."

Claire sighs and starts braiding a tiny strand of hair. "That makes me feel a little better. I was feeling like such a jerk because I didn't have the right words for any of it. I didn't know what to say to Kat at the funeral, and she didn't seem like she wanted to talk to us, so I didn't know if we did something wrong. If I did something wrong. But I also get the wanting to be alone part." She sighs. "Then, in the car, I didn't know what to say to you guys, and no one said anything, so I thought maybe we weren't supposed to say anything. So my mind drifted to my apartment. I mean my old apartment." She finishes that braid and starts in on another section. I have no idea how her fingers move that fast. "Mom's moving this weekend."

"Oh, right." I turn away from the keys and toward my friends. "Are you all right with that? Do you like the new place? Did your mom send pics?"

"She's not exactly the Instagram type." Claire shakes her head. "Plus, only organized people like you gather and e-mail pictures, Han. She did tell me the name of the place. I Googled it so I could check it out. Pretty basic, one-bedroom, beige apartment." Claire looks past me at the piano. "It's pretty weird. I feel almost homeless. It's stupid, really." She shakes her head. "I'll just be there over breaks and stuff anyway. I'll float around. I might try to stay here at school over the summer, if I can find a job and cheap rent."

"You could live with me over the summer!" Palmer shrieks. "That would be so amazing!"

"Or me!" I add. "How fun would it be if we were all in Columbus all summer long, together! All four of us!

Although you'd have to put up with Sammie following you around and Owen wanting to show you ten jillion Lego creations. I love them, but sometimes they can drive me as crazy as a daisy." I sit next to Claire on the couch.

"Just like Tia," Palmer says. "She and I got in a brawl before I left because she wanted to keep the boots I traded her until Thanksgiving! She literally wouldn't trade back, so now I'm stuck with these for another three weeks! Plus, they kill my feet. Total bug!" Palmer kicks her foot in the air, displaying one of the gorgeous leather boots.

"I would kill for those boots," Claire says.

"Maybe I'll give them to you. That would show Tia." Palmer does a little happy dance and sits down with us. "But then, what if she never gave me back my black Tory Burch boots? Enormous bug! I'd need a giant can of bug spray to deal with the problem."

I squirt an imaginary spray bottle and make a spraying sound. "Why do they hurt your feet?" I ask.

"They're a size too small. I don't mind squeezing my feet into them for a few days. I mean, fashion before comfort, but three weeks, come on!"

Claire and I laugh at Palmer. She is a piece of work. But I love her.

Claire leans in, which is a good sign; she always seems a few feet removed. "So, if I move in with one of you, is it BYOB? Bring your own bug spray, or do you provide that for your guests?"

"Ha!" Palmer laughs and swats Claire's knee. Then she sits up extra tall. "True confession time. I know we're all worried about Kat, and I really am, but I'm the biggest jerk of all. Because you know what I've been thinking about? I've been thinking about the funeral, of course, everyone's sad and you're not even supposed to cheer them up. Ugh." She waves her hands around. "But I'm mainly thinking about how relieved I was to get out of that church and away from Keegan. Can you believe he was there? Can you believe he hugged me like that, at the end?"

"Who was that cute guy sitting next to Keegan?" I ask, picturing the row of boys sitting behind us. "You know, the one with the blue-and-white-striped shirt. The blonde?"

"That's Craig." Palmer tosses her glossy hair like a shampoo commercial.

"So are you guys over over?" Claire asks.

Palmer scrunches up her mouth. "Yeah."

The silence returns as we all fall back into our own problems, our own thoughts. It's not awkward anymore, though, because we've shard them, all of us but Kat. "It's weird not having Kat here," I say. "I know it's only been a couple of months, but you guys get me, like, really get me. I feel like we're all long-lost soul mates or cousins, like we've always lived together." I lace my fingers with Palmer's on one side of me and Claire's on the other. "So to think of Kat not studying until she passes out tonight and not sprinting off to soccer at the crack of dawn. I can't even picture it. Or not picture it. You know?"

CHAPTER TWENTY-THREE – KAT

I FOLLOW THE *WHOOSHING* BLAST to the mudroom where Mama sprays Febreze in an old suitcase.

"Go on, now. Get yourself goin', girl. Daddy's takin' you back in an hour or so. I found this suitcase to send some warm clothes with you back to school along with your other things. I'll never get used to this Yankee weather." Mama shakes her head and sprays some more.

Part of me longs to hide under my covers forever. The other part wants to run away from this house and all the memories, anything to keep the pain locked away. Mama's resolve with the suitcase gives me my route without having to weigh the choices.

I have no idea how long I hibernated in my room. I only remember coming out for pizza and peeing. I feel mussed and sweaty and lethargic from my post funeral mega-slumber. I apparently drooled too, which was obvious by the puddle on my pillow. I need a very long, very hot shower.

I turn the water to scalding so it can break through the numbness encasing me. The heat works on my skin until it penetrates the dull layer I've built around myself, like the pads hockey players wear to muffle the blows. My nerves celebrate the sensation. I've felt dead for the past I don't know how many days. How long has it been since Alex died? It feels like it was last night. Like these last days have been one long nightmare and this emptiness, this aching is the only thing I've ever known.

I thrust my face into the pounding spray. I scrub my scalp, attempting to scour away the film of darkness and despair.

"*Ahhhh!*" The sting of the razor slicing into my leg makes me grit my teeth and flap my free hand. It hurts like crazy, but I laugh. I feel it! It feels good to feel something, to be alive!

Can I say that? Is it all right if I feel good to be alive when Alex is not?

I abruptly turn off the water to punish myself for the enjoyment of its warmth. I grab my turquoise towel and marvel at how soft it feels on my skin. I dab a wad of toilet paper where scarlet blood drips from my calf, vibrant and daring. I slather raspberry lotion all over my body. The sweet, fruity scent wakes up my senses, which feel like they've been turned off for way too long.

I hear Mama opening and closing closet doors. I stand still. I don't want her to peek her head in and ask why I screamed, or see if I'm packed or anything. I don't want to run into her in the hall and wonder if she'll yell at me or ignore me. It's all too hard. If I leave I won't have to face her, but if I leave I have to do it all alone.

Can I do this?

My thoughts float to the faces of my roommates and of Nicholas.

So, not completely alone after all. I nod to myself, willing myself to finish getting ready. As I pull my hair back with my favorite Nike headband, the one I wear on game days, I imagine the soccer field. My breath catches.

Soccer.

That's something I *can* do, something I *need* to do. Somehow, I'll make myself do the rest, so I can play.

I pack like a robot, taking the things I brought with me for what was supposed to be a relaxing three-day weekend, but turned into a week of torment and trauma.

Mama hugs me at the doorstep. "Study hard, darlin'," she whispers. I squeeze her tighter, not able to let go.

"Why don't you come with us?" I ask.

She shakes her head severely and backs away.

"Mama?"

"Go on, now. Your daddy has to drive you all the way there and back tonight. That's five hours for him. You better get a move on it."

I nod and obey, climbing into Daddy's car with my bags. But I want to tell Mama how much I love her even though we haven't been talking, and that I'm really, really scared to go back, but worried about what will happen if I don't. Like what if they kick me off the team? Or bench me for the season? Because she used to give me words of wisdom when I was worried. Lately, I'm lucky if she gives me any words at all. I'm worried sick about leaving her and Daddy at home. So much left unsaid. But too hard to say it.

As we back down the driveway, I wave to Mama, who gives a quick wave, then heads inside. I picture Alex waving beside her, then following Mama, trailing after her, making sure she'll be all right by herself. I feel better, knowing he's looking after her.

Daddy and I drive in silence for a while, letting the radio fill the empty air between us.

After about an hour Daddy says in his resonant voice, "Kat, you know, this is really hard on Mama. She loves you. It's not that she didn't want to come, it's just—" He clears his throat. "She needs some time. Which brings us to Thanksgiving. It's comin' up, you know, and Mama and I've been talking about what we'll do."

A shiver crawls from my headband down to my gym shoes. I hug myself to ward off the chill. Thanksgiving's always been our family's biggest holiday. We start the day with Mama's famous cheese grits, end it with her pecan pie, and fill in between with our annual Turkey Bowl. I always make waffles while Alex squeezes fresh orange juice. After an enormous brunch, he and I take a four-pack of Hanes XL T-shirts and sit down at the kitchen table with paint pens to create jerseys for our football teams. It's always him and Mama versus Daddy and me. Last year we were the Pumpkin Prize. Mama and Alex were the Cranberry Crunchers. After the game we snuggle on couches to watch *Charlie Brown's Thanksgiving* while the thick, herb-filled aroma of turkey stuffed with cornbread floats through the house. We feast and stay up late watching college football drinking hot apple cider and eating pecan pie.

I feel like apple cider drips out of my eyes and into a big empty turkey roaster in my stomach, splashing with each warm, sweet drop. I'm physically whipped and emotionally drained. I turn my head toward the window in a lame attempt to hide the river of tears pouring down my face.

I drum my thumb ring on the armrest. "Alex probably already had his and Mama's team name picked out. Did he tell you what it was?"

"Nope." Daddy shakes his head. "Kat, Mama can't do Thanksgiving. Not like that. It's . . . too hard." He squeezes my hand across the console.

"What?" I squeak, wiping the tears with the back of my other hand.

"It wouldn't be the same. It's too soon. Mama's gonna visit her sister in Alabama. I'm takin' a business trip to Barcelona." His voice is methodical.

"What about me?" I squeeze Daddy's hand tighter for support as I feel myself free falling into nothingness. No Thanksgiving. No Alex. Mama gone. Daddy gone.

"I haven't forgotten my promise." A tiny crinkle forms around Daddy's eyes.

The last time Daddy went to Spain, he promised he'd take us some time, Alex and me, if he ever went back. I imagine the buzz of a hundred voices speaking in Spanish in the marketplace and street performers juggling fire and doing flips, just like Daddy described.

"I'll be buried in meetings, but I'm sure you'd find plenty to do. I hope you'll join me."

I look into Daddy's face, his face that looks so much like Alex's would have looked had he ever gotten the chance to grow up. Tears drop by the teaspoonful from his emerald eyes.

"Really?" I eek.

Daddy nods.

"I'll come. I really want to come."

CHAPTER TWENTY-FOUR – HANNAH

I STRETCH SIDEWAYS AND REACH for my phone.

"Hi, Mommy. Thanks for calling me back. Your Hannah Banana misses you."

"What do you need, dear?" I can tell from her voice, Mom sees right through my schmoozeathon.

"I started working on a paper at home and saved it to your laptop, but forgot to e-mail it to myself. Could you send it?"

"Sure. What's the file name?"

"Hastate. Bad, right? It's some kind of triangular plant, and the unfortunate topic of my Botany assignment."

"Consider it done."

"And could you pretty please send my lavender sweater, you know the super cozy one?"

"Hannah." Mom sighs.

"Pretty please with sugar on top?" I walk around the dorm room, putting a coffee mug back on the rack, folding a pair of Claire's jeans, and stuffing two granola bar wrappers in the trash can.

"Okay, honey, it's just not going to be until later this week."

"But it got so cold all of a sudden. I'm freezing down here." I rub my hands up and down my arms to make my point, even though Mom can't see me.

"You are not freezing, and I'm sorry, but the contractor will be here in five minutes and I have to pick out tile, measure for handrails, and meet with the realtor." Humongous sigh from Mom.

"Contractor? Realtor?" I grab a handful of candy corn from the cute little pumpkin bowl I set out on our coffee table.

"Dad was supposed to call you." Another large sigh from Mom. "I thought that's why you left a message. We're moving Grampa in with us. So we need to sell his house, make the playroom into a handicapped-accessible bedroom for him, and make alterations to the downstairs bathroom too."

"Grampa's moving in with us? Hooray!"

"You really didn't know?" Mom sounds tired.

"Um, I got a message from Dad, but didn't really listen to it. Sorry." I bite the yellow top off a candy corn. "But really? That is so way better than that stinky old nursing home. It gave me the creeps. I'm so excited! Is Grampa giddy? When's he moving in?" I gnaw off the orange part and save the pure sugar white tip for last.

"The nursing home wasn't stinky, but it was expensive . . . and lonely. I think we'll all be happier if he's with us, including Grampa. Our goal is to have him here for Thanksgiving, but that's going to take a small miracle. You can't say anything yet, Hannah. It's going to be a surprise for him."

"It *was* too stinky! Mom, it smelled like pee! And Thanksgiving! Yay! I'll be there for his move-in day. We can make peppermint bark and do crosswords and everything." I eat another candy corn in the same order. "So Grampa doesn't know. And you're selling his house.

Um, shouldn't someone tell him? And what does O think about the playroom?"

"Owen's a little concerned about where he'll put all his Legos, but Dad and I promised him we'll have the contractor build a special table in his room for them. One more thing to add to the list. And we've talked this all through. Grampa can't manage his house, Hannah. He's going to be in a wheelchair for the long haul. It's truly for the best."

The doorbell rings from Mom's end of the phone.

"That's the contractor, honey. I've gotta run. We'll chat more later. And from now on, listen to messages from Dad and me, okay?"

"Sure. Sorry. Love you, Mom. Pet Ziggy for me."

"Love you too."

"Oh, oh, Mommy, dearest, please don't forget my paper and the sweater, okay? I promise to help oodles on Turkey Day."

"Okay, okay. Love you."

"Love you too."

Claire shuffles into our family room in sweats and a cami, yawning. "Morning," she mumbles, glancing at the clock, which reads 10:45 a.m.

"How can you sleep so late? Doesn't your brain just swirl with stuff to do?" I plop on the couch with my laptop, e-mailing Mom a reminder to send me those things so she doesn't forget when she's done with the contractor. She sounded pretty distracted.

"How can you just wake up?" Claire stretches and grabs a Tazo from our fridge. "My brain spins so much at night it completely shuts off in the morning." She closes her eyes tight, then opens them wide. "I have, like, five minutes to get ready for my eleven o'clock. Do we have any granola bars left?"

"So you're the granola wrapper culprit." I eye her. "Will you grab lunch with me after your class?"

"Can't. I have an eleven, a twelve, then a two."

"When do you eat?"

"Whenever. I just grab food in the dining hall in between one of my classes or after. Whatever works."

"You know the breakfast there is super yum. You should join Palmer and me tomorrow." I'm guessing Claire didn't hear me, because she darted into the bathroom. How does she do that? How can she not know when she'll eat? I'd go bonkers.

"Sorry about the wrappers." Claire pulls her hair in a loose side pony and digs a bar from the box in our communal food crate. "Where are Palm and Kat?"

"Palmer had an eight. Then she was headed to the library to work on her article for the magazine because it's due tonight. Kat ran off early to soccer. I'm uber-worried about her." I pace back and forth.

Claire nods with her mouth full.

"And sorry I totally spaced about your noon class. I had everyone's schedules memorized, but I've got way too much going on in here." I tap my forehead. "How about dinner?"

"Sure. After ballet. Meet you at our usual table. Any idea what they're serving?" Claire pulls a flowy pink cardigan around her body. "Did Kat say anything this morning? She barely nodded at us when she showed up last night."

"Lasagna. Which sounds decent. And I just saw her for a nanosecond. She literally ran out of here. It didn't seem like a good time to bring up her brother dying and how she was doing with that." I crack my gum.

"That's her usual gig in the mornings, though, right?" Claire peeks in the mirror and slathers on pearly lip gloss. "Isn't she always dashing to soccer? I get the feeling she likes to sleep almost as much as I do, but she gets up for soccer. I'd get up for ballet. That's about it."

"Yeah. I just don't know how she's going to do it. How do you go to class and sports and stuff right after a tragedy? Like nothing happened?"

Claire sucks in her breath and looks down.

An instant pit fills my stomach. "Sorry. I mean, your brother didn't die, but you had to jump back into everything after . . . after what happened. Why can't I say anything right?" I know my freckles must be beet red. Poor Claire. She's fragile enough without me bombarding her with insensitive comments in the morning.

"It's all right." She shakes her head. "Kat can do this. She's strong. But she's going to need us. Big-time."

"Mega big-time. It makes the drama about my grampa moving in seem like nothing."

"He's moving in—to your house?" Claire gives her lashes a coat of mascara.

"Mom just told me on the phone." I tap my purple phone case. "He's moving in on Thanksgiving, but he doesn't even know yet. How weird will that be? I guess I get to see him then. Did you decide if you're going to Detroit for Thanksgiving?"

"I think so. I'll tell you all about it at dinner." Claire grabs her bag and calls, "Bye" as she dashes down the hall.

CHAPTER TWENTY-FIVE – KAT

AFTER PUNCHING THE "UP" ARROWS on my phone until the music is so loud the bass vibrations drown out all my thoughts, I escape my room before my roommates can bombard me with questions. I head to the fields where my teammates set water bottles by the bench and bat balls back and forth, trying to warm up in the chilly October morning air.

Turning off my music, I trade the melodies for the comforting thud of leather shoes on leather balls, hollow and solid. The trainers put up some sort of net—it almost looks like a Ping-Pong net—except instead of being on a table top, it stretches across the dark green blades of dew-covered grass.

Three guys stroll toward the men's fields. Their backs are to me, but the middle one has broad shoulders and almost white hair in a buzz cut like Alex's. I hold my breath.

He's wearing a gray T-shirt and navy blue gym shorts, like a million pairs Alex has stuffed in his drawers. My heart patters faster, faster. He's taller than the guy on the right and shorter than the guy on the left. The guy on the right is definitely Dave Silverman, the starting fullback.

"Alex!" I whisper scream. His name scrapes my throat. I step toward him, but the blonde turns and lightly punches Dave, and it's not Alex at all.

Of course it's not.

It couldn't be.

It's Aaron Bissler, a junior soccer player. I feel woozy and so tired I think my eyes will snap shut. My heart pounds, but I use the throb to push the pain back, away from me back into its cage. I sway backward, but steady myself when my teammate Emily bumps into me, tugged forward by a black-and-white cocker spaniel on a leash.

"Sorry, Kat, my little puppy here has a mind of his own, don't you?"

I look down at the dog, then back to Aaron Bissler, proving to myself it is NOT Alex. Thankfully, there's no sign of Tony, the mysterious bad boy on the men's team, the other boy I kissed. He really understands how I feel about soccer, but I don't think he'd understand about Alex. I don't' even think I could tell him about Alex. No way I could deal with him too. I remind myself to breathe. The locker around my heart clicks shut, tighter this time. There is safety in keeping my emotions in there. Then I can't hurt, right?

I lose myself in the dog, focusing on anything besides the fact I thought I just saw my dead brother—that my brother is dead.

I kneel. "Well, aren't you the cutest thing?" I pat the pooch's back. "What's your name, feller?"

"Domino," Emily coos, rubbing his neck.

"He's adorable, aren't you? Aren't you?" I ask the furry body with floppy ears, grateful for the diversion.

"Thanks." Emily smiles. "He just wouldn't stay in my apartment this morning. Do you think Coach'll mind?"

"Who could mind your precious little self," I ask Domino, stroking the silkiness of his fur.

"Stretches, ladies!" Coach DeLuca booms. Coach D is short and strong and Italian. Where he comes from soccer is the national game and it's called futbol. He refuses to call it soccer. He takes the game more seriously than life itself, and when he talks we listen.

I release my clutch on Domino and jog to the center circle of the field.

Our captain, Olivia, stands in the middle, and her peppy voice belts, "Right leg, one, two, three, four, five."

"Let's hear it!" Coach commands. The lilt in his thick accent, the smell of freshly mowed grass, the chorus of my teammates counting, the blue sky spreading up and out endlessly consumes me.

Our volume increases several decibels. "Six, seven, eight . . ."

Adrenaline courses through my veins. I count as loudly as my voice can shout. I feel my vocal chords resonating in my throat. This is where I am home. This is where I am me. Where nothing else matters.

When stretches are over, Coach strides to the low net. "We are not going to play futbol quite yet. We're going to play folleyball."

"Folleyball? What you talkin' about, Coachie?" Latoya, our center forward, asks, twirling a braid. She is the only one of us who could get away with that.

"You will start us, no?" He motions for Latoya to stand behind the net. "You serve the ball with your foot, and somebody from this side will kick it back, and so on and so on. I do not ever want to see the ball fall to the ground. It is all about control, ladies! Control!"

This is Coach DeLuca's favorite line. It echoes through my head like the lyrics of a familiar song. "It's all about control."

"We will count into groups of ones and twos!"

We count off. We take sides. We volley the ball back and forth focusing on control and placement. My whole head is in the game. I send the ball across the net straight to Emily's foot exactly where I want it to go. She drops the ball down from her thigh to her laces, sailing it back to my chest. I deaden the ball in one fluid motion, feeling the familiar thud. The impact against my body is solid and real and sends a zing up to the roots of my hair and down to the ends of my toenails.

After this drill, we run sprints up and down the field. I push my legs faster and faster. I've been out, and I don't want Coach to think I've been slacking. I run, and my heart wants to jump out of my mouth to give itself a break. I feel it in my throat keeping me from breathing, then bouncing back down to my chest and tightening.

"Enough," Coach Baker, our assistant, calls.

I'll do whatever he says, especially if it means taking a break and breathing for a minute. I stand on the white line painted on the grass and pant like Domino, feeling my shoulders lunging forward and back.

"Starters, stay here. The rest of you, on Field Two with me," Coach Baker says. He's younger and kind of nerdy with his glasses and a lopsided smile, but he means business on the pitch. I start toward Field Two, but Coach Baker stops me.

"Sorry about your brother, Kat. We missed you out here."

I hold my breath. No one had asked me yet where I've been or why I've been gone or why I came back today. I thought maybe everyone was too busy with warm-ups, or maybe nobody knew what happened.

A tiny part of me wanted someone to acknowledge it, because it's who I am now. But most of me was relieved no one asked how it feels to have your brother die or your mama flip out or stay in a dark bed for days on end. But here it comes. I'm not ready. I squeeze my hands into fists. *Please, Coach, don't go into this*, I silently plead. It helps me ignore the pain if no one says anything. I look down at the grass, blade after blade entangled with the next blade.

But all Coach says is, "You all right, then?"

I nod and exhale slowly.

"Anything we can do?"

"Let me play." I try to say it without my voice shaking too much. Playing is my only hope at staying stable, at staying sane.

"Good to have you back!" He pats my back, and we stride off to Field Two. Now it's done. He acknowledged it, but didn't make me talk. I can do this. It's all about control.

CHAPTER TWENTY-SIX – PALMER

I PUSH MY GLASSES UP my nose. I wear them instead of my contacts when I'm in serious writing mode, very Lois Lane.

My fingers dance across my keyboard, tapping letters into words and words into complete thoughts. They stop. I sit up straight and square my shoulders.

Delete, delete, delete.

This article has to be good. No, perfect. It's my first feature; well, it will be if it gets accepted for the student magazine. It was a huge deal to be selected for the staff, but that doesn't insure I get to write. Some people have been on the magazine for three years, and they're still selling ads and organizing layouts, which might be fine for them, but I want to write and write and write some more.

This issue comes out on Halloween. It will be filled with stories about candy and costumes and campus traditions. But the story I was assigned is a serious piece on dealing with grief. If you ask me, I got the spookiest task of all. I suspect the editors made it ultra hard as a test, to see if I can write or not. I'm starting to wonder myself.

If I maintain an unbiased journalist's perspective, I end up sounding cold and insensitive to such an emotional topic, which is not okay. But if I let myself think about what happened to Alex—I mean, what really happened—I shake. Sometimes I get mad at Tia, like with the whole boot hostage situation, but really, if she just vanished from the earth, if she died, how would I feel?

I picture my sister the last time I saw her, right after Alex's funeral. Was I really mad about the boots or just wound up about seeing Keegan?

I click on the e-mail icon on the bottom of my screen.

Tia, I'm so sorry about yelling at you. You know I love you, sis. Keep my boots safe, and I'll see you at Thanksgiving. Be ready to bake pumpkin pies and shop till you drop on Black Friday. Xoxo, Palm

I love the zwooping sound when an e-mail sends. My conscience slightly eased, I click back on my story.

Loss – n. the harm or suffering caused by losing or being lost

What kind of definition defines itself with the word it's defining? But it's true, isn't it? My relationship with Keegan—the loss isn't the fact that it's over as much as the "harm and suffering" caused by it being over.

By the end of Alex's funeral I was sobbing. I wanted to hold Kat tight and safe so she couldn't hurt. I also wanted to escape, to get away from all the sadness, but Keegan slid out of the pew behind me and held *me*, as if it were his duty to protect me. Old habits die hard. His arms around me used to be my drug of choice, but now I realize he's toxic for me.

I'm finally to the point where I get that. The fights, the emotional roller coaster. All the misunderstandings and disagreements and accusations are not healthy. So why do I crave his warmth and strength, the security he used to be? Why do I keep going back?

My fingers fly now, my coral-colored nails pouring my feelings of loss into my laptop. Not that I understand what it's like when someone you love dies, but I get the loss part. And it seems to transfer perfectly. What you thought you had and the hole it leaves when it's no longer there—good holes and bad holes, big holes and small holes, crucial holes and trivial holes, so many holes, which leave a person feeling empty.

I immerse myself in my article, unaware of anything but the words as they form like colorful solid shapes in my head and zip from my brain to my fingers to the keyboard, where they appear on my screen. I stop thinking about Keegan and how cute my glasses look and even about how Kat's going to get through this. My objective is to tell this story. To make my point. By the time I'm done, my head feels clearer, my heart stronger. Writing is therapy.

I run the spelling and grammar check, reread my Word document in my head, to make sure it's perfect, and push Send.

Zwoop.

"Hey, Palmer, isn't it?"

I blink to clear my screen-dazed eyes and turn. "Yes."

The dark-haired editor from the magazine, Michael, smiles at me, a five o-clock shadow covering his pronounced chin, even though it's not quite lunchtime. "I didn't know you wore glasses. You look good in them. Intelligent." He nods. His voice is deep, like a full-grown man's. "I heard you're submitting a feature for consideration this month."

"Thanks." I smile. He said "intelligent," not "hot." I like the sounds of that—a lot. "I just pushed Send."

"Really?" He strokes his stubbly chin. "Can't wait to read it. I interviewed that alum who's running for governor in the election for my piece."

"What was he like?" I swivel in my chair.

"Typical politician." Michael shrugs. "Join me for lunch? I'll tell you all about it."

"Sounds great. Give me a minute to power off."

I knew writing was good for me. I just didn't know how good.

CHAPTER TWENTY-SEVEN – CLAIRE

OUTSIDE THE DOORS OF THE dining hall, I pause. Part of me wants to grab a slice of pizza by myself and eat in the privacy of our room. But I promised Hannah, and her whole mood seems to hinge on whether we dine together or not, which is strange for me. Mom and I usually did our own thing, sometimes connecting, sometimes not, very fend-for-yourself. It is nice how much Hannah wants me here, wants us all here.

"Hey, girls." I plop my tray down on the table across from Palmer and next to Kat. I didn't know if she'd be here. I'm so proud of her for making the effort. She's so strong. I hug her, but she stiffens. I pull away, understanding if she doesn't want to be touched.

Then Kat whispers, "Claire," and squeezes me back, just for a second, and I know it's okay. She smells like freshly mown grass and fallen leaves.

"You okay?" I ask.

Kat taps her thumb ring on the table. "I've been better."

We all let out nervous laughs, shrill and tinny.

"There you are," Hannah says, sitting down with a bowl of ice cream from the soft-serve machine.

"Just in time for dessert?" I half smile, hoping Hannah's not mad I'm late. "I wanted to do one last round of pique turns across the floor. They were optional, but, like, required if you want a part in *The Nutcracker*, and optional if you don't care if you get cast."

"Ooh! I love *The Nutcracker*! When are tryouts?" Palmer digs her spoon into Hannah's ice cream. "I could write a story about it for the winter edition of the magazine."

Hannah opens her mouth like she's about to scold me for being late, but then her expression softens. "Try the lasagna. It's pretty good."

I chew my mouthful of cheesy pasta. "Mmm. It is good. Really good." I take another bite. "Tryouts are next week. I'm really nervous." I'm also nervous to say anything to Kat, but someone has to say something. I bite my lip. "Kat, so, you're okay? I was praying for you all day."

"Thanks."

"You'll do great, Claire." Hannah sinks her spoon into a mound of vanilla swirls. "And me too, Kat. Praying for you, that is. We barely saw you last night, just, like, for one second when you and your dad came in and then you crashed." Hannah cringes at her own words and throws her hands over her face. "Oh my gosh, Kat, I so didn't mean to say crashed. I meant to say you went straight to bed. And you just had to dive back into everything today. I mean . . ." Hannah scoops ice cream into her mouth so she doesn't have to finish her sentence.

"I was praying for you too." Palmer nods.

Kat pushes back her half-eaten tray. "Thanks, y'all. Really." She tightens her ponytail. "I just don't know. I mean, practice was great. It felt amazing to be back on the pitch, like I could really do this, ya know? But classes were crazy hard. I bumped into some guy, and I swore he shaves with Edge shaving cream, which is what Alex uses . . . used." She looks down and swallows. When she looks back up, her green eyes are wet.

A lump forms in my throat. Feeling for Kat, for how hard it is to talk about the nightmare, but it being unavoidable if you want to keep going, I place my hand on her arm lightly, and when she twitches, I pull away.

"So, he smelled exactly like Alex, and I swore I sniffed him. Like this." Kat scrunches up her nose and sniffs like a hound on the hunt.

I laugh loudly and cover my mouth. "Sorry."

"It's all right." Kat smiles. "I'm just a wreck. That dude must think I'm insane. Maybe I am insane."

"Nice to know I'm not the only one walking around in a daze." I unwind my long braid from my bun. "It's hard when it's still there, in your brain, ya know?" I look to Kat.

She nods.

Go ahead, an inner voice urges, but I am so not good at speaking up. *You can do this. Kat needs you.*

"But, hey, guys?" I ask, feeling my voice shake.

Palmer looks up from a text. "What?"

"You know our Bible study?"

"I'm so glad you brought that up." Hannah beams, like I might have even made up for being late. "We were holding them Monday nights, but the last two weeks"—she looks at Kat—"have been, well, unpredictable." Hannah leans forward. "So, can we have it tonight, or if you guys aren't prepared, that is completely fine, we could schedule it for tomorrow."

"How about we just get back on track on Monday?" Palmer slides her phone in her purse. "Then we can all be back in the swing." She shrugs. "Ya know?"

Hannah looks around nodding at everyone, her eyes twinkling. "Okay, next Monday. Thanks, Claire, for bringing it up."

So much for what I was going to say.

Try again, God urges. *Say it, for Kat.*

Right.

My knees bounce under the table.

"Uh, Monday's good, but what I was going to say was . . ." This is harder than I thought it would be. Why am I so shy around my own roommates? "Well, my counselor suggested I write one thing I'm grateful for each day in a notebook." I put down my fork because my hand is quivering.

"I'm so glad you went to see a counselor." Hannah's eyes light up. "Is it through the program I told you about? The one the college provides?"

"Yeah. Exactly. Thanks." I take a sip of water. "You know I've struggled with what Phillip did to me, and you guys have been the only way I've been able to stay in school, let alone stay sane—like you talking me into seeing someone." I smile at Hannah, because even though she keeps interrupting, she doesn't know I'm trying to spit something out, and I *am* glad she suggested the counselor. "And I'm so thankful, so grateful God gave me you as roommates." I run my fingers through my hair so it falls back at my shoulders. "I mean, I could have ended up with some really mean girls, or with someone who didn't care, but I'm so blessed." I look down. When I look back up, Palmer, Kat, and Hannah are all looking at me. Not like I'm crazy, but like they want to hear what I'll say next.

"So I took her advice and wrote how thankful I was for the three of you in big, bold letters at the top of my journal, so when I was feeling an anxiety attack I'd have something positive to think about."

"Aww. You're so sweet, Claire Bear." Palmer blows me a kiss across the table.

"What a cool idea." Hannah wipes her mouth with a napkin. "Why didn't I think of that?"

"You thought of the counselor." I undo the plaits of my braid. "So, it kinda worked. The next day I was walking back from class and felt like I might literally be smothered in the crowd of people, but I pictured where I wrote your names, hot pink ink and all, and remembered I was headed back to you guys, and that helped me not freak out."

I twirl the piece of hair tighter and tighter. "So, the next day I wrote something else I was thankful for, and just kept doing it."

I look at Kat, who's staring pretty intently at her plate.

"I was thinking if it helped me, it might help all of us. We're all a bit out of whack." I shake my head, allowing my hair to free itself completely from its sections. "And then we could share them at Bible study."

"Love, love, love!" Palmer tilts her head. "I'm ready to go right now." She sits up super straight. "I'm thankful I finished my article for the magazine today." She claps her hands together.

"Yay you!" Hannah says.

"That's great, Palm." Kat nods.

"And the cute editor took me to lunch!" Palmer raises her eyebrows.

"Double yay." I laugh.

"Unfair!" Hannah fake scowls. "You get all the boys. Okay, my turn, my turn." Hannah wiggles so much in her seat, she might knock over what's left of her ice cream. "I'm thankful for the most awesome possum roomies, and Bible study, and candy corn. Oh my gosh, I love that stuff, and this is the only time of year you can find it. I brought all these yummy flavors from home, like caramel apple candy corn and chocolate candy corn."

"Chocolate candy corn? Get out! Where are you hiding it?" Palmer demands.

"It's all in the dorm. Let's have a taste test when we get back to our room." Hannah grins.

Palmer claps again.

Kat drums her thumbs on the table. I'm guessing she'll need awhile to come up with something she's thankful for. I know it was days after my counselor suggested it to me that I came up with anything. She surprises me by blurting, "I'm thankful I'm going to Barcelona with my daddy over Thanksgiving."

"Get out!" Palmer shouts. "So unfair. I've never left the U.S. ever!"

"Did you say something about Barca?" Tony, the guy with the combo buzz cut and dreadlocks from the men's soccer team, sits down next to Kat. "They are the best team in the world. Messi is amazing. Did you say you watched them? 'Cause I didn't know they played last night." He might as well be speaking Spanish, because I don't have a clue what he's talking about.

Kat's face turns as red as the tomato sauce on my plate.

"No," Hannah says coldly. "Kat said she's going to Barcelona. The city. In Spain."

"Cool." Tony stuffs an entire piece of garlic bread in his mouth in one bite. "You girls all ready for your game this weekend?"

Kat smiles. "I hope so. If we could only get Messi to guest play, we'd be all set."

I stick my fork in my lasagna, hoping Barcelona is the magic potion to heal Kat and reminding myself to ask her later who Messi is.

CHAPTER TWENTY-EIGHT – KAT

I'VE MADE IT THROUGH TWO entire weeks of school. Each day, each class, each minute. In the mornings I feel like I'm pulling an anvil off my eyelids. I tug imaginary thick, metal, heavy chains to raise myself out of bed, and then flee my room before my roommates get too personal. I feel bad, but it's easier to stay by myself.

At practice I pounce on the ball. Attacking it again and again, honing my emotions on that leather sphere.

In classes, I burn my energy struggling to pay attention. I bite my tongue, raise my hand, and twirl my rings, anything to stay mentally awake through lectures on variables, *Don Quixote*, and World War II. Why does everything take such calculated effort? Everything I used to just do, now I have to plan and execute.

Like today. My folks drove down to Clarkston to see my soccer game. But it's not as easy as that. I know Daddy dragged Mama here, and he only did that 'cause he's feeling guilty. So I'm feeling guilty that they came, and well, it's just one giant mess. Not to mention we haven't talked, not really, since I came back to school. I don't even know what to say to them.

"Hey, sugar." Daddy plants a kiss on my forehead.

"Kat." Mama barely reaches her arms around my torso, then quickly retracts. Like she's required to hug me. Like she's reading a script. But she is here. It's been two weeks since I've seen her. When we touched she felt warmer and more solid than I imagined she would.

"Thanks for comin' to see me play." I nod at both my folks, wanting them to know how much it means.

"I don't know how you can be so consumed with soccer when Alex will never get to swim again," Mama whispers, but not quietly enough.

The words stab like the sword of a fencer thrusting my heart again and again. I know Alex'll never swim again! Does she think I don't realize that every time I see a blond head and broad shoulders sauntering across campus? I know he's not coming back, but *I* am still here!

I stomp past her and shut myself in the bedroom. I slam the door for effect. I want to attack Mama, but I know my feelings are better channeled toward the Hornets.

I slide on my shin guards, socks, and cleats. I hit my sternum, that place where I've protected my heart. I won't let Mama's words go there. There's no room for them. I grab my water bottle. Then the lovely sensation of butterfly wings dances in my stomach. I'm never sure exactly when they'll arrive, but the fluttering comes before each game. They almost chase away the grinding in my stomach from Mama's remark.

Almost.

I walk back into our main room, right past where Palmer is attempting small talk. "So, how long was your drive?" she says.

"Not bad. Just a little over two hours, I'd guess," Daddy says distractedly.

Hannah darts around straightening stacks of magazines and shoving textbooks on shelves. Claire sits crisscrossed on the floor braiding her hair.

"We're going to drop off some things for Nicholas at his dorm from his folks, and then we'll meet you down at the fields in time for the game, sugar." Daddy taps me on the back. "Good luck. We'll be cheering for you."

Mama's next to him, lips tight, staring into space.

Claire silently stands and hooks her arm in mine. It makes me feel stronger, strong enough to speak. "I'm fixin' to head to the fields. I have to be there early."

"Ready, steady, go." Hannah grabs her jacket.

"Y'all don't have to come now. It won't start for an hour."

"We could all use the fresh air." Hannah nods decisively.

And it's settled. I can't help but think Hannah's stepping in and mothering me when my own mama wouldn't. I shake my head, overwhelmed. These girls are good for me.

"I just need a sec with the mirror." Palmer grins. "You never know who you'll run into."

I nod, staring at a spot on the carpet.

Once outside Palmer waves her arms frantically. "What the heck was all that about? No offense, Kat, but your mom was way out of line."

Claire doesn't say a word but squeezes my arm a little tighter, like she's holding me up.

"I know, right? I felt so awkward. I didn't have a clue what to say. They are your parents, and they did come to visit, so it would have been inappropriate for me to say what was on my mind." Hannah pops her gum.

"Yeah, sorry. She's kinda been like that." I cough to clear my throat. "Y'all won't be upset if I listen to my tunes, will you? There're a couple of songs I listen to before games, to get me in the right mind-set, ya know?"

Before they can protest, I unwind my earbuds and tuck them in my ears. I think Hannah's trying to say something else, but I swirl my thumb around the dial, cranking up "Rock What You Got" by Superchick.

The sun warms my skin, and the scent of grass works like smelling salts for my soul. I bop my head back and forth to the music, sensing the swing of my ponytail, while I shake Mama's words and everything else from my brain.

At the pitch, Claire unhooks her arm and whispers in my ear, "Love you, Kat." I almost forgot she was here.

"Love you too, Bear," I whisper back, clicking off my iPod.

Hannah squeezes me. "Knock their socks off! Or maybe that should be knock their shin guards off." She giggles. "That would be so funny."

"That would be funny."

"Stick it to them, sister." Palmer clasps my hand.

"Thanks. Y'all are the best."

I ditch my roommates for my teammates. We stretch and pass the ball. The Hornets, dressed in green and gold, do similar drills at the other end of the field. I bounce up and down on my toes. A paper white butterfly darts past the goal, and I wonder if it flew out of my stomach.

I sit the bench for the first half of the game. I don't mind, except I want to get out there and play so badly I almost explode. I don't want to bring up why I missed those practices, so I take my discipline on the bench and grit my teeth. But my toes bounce, and I lean so far forward in my seat I almost fall on my face.

Halfway through the second half, the score is 1–0 Hornets.

Coach shouts, "Kat!" and points to the field. I dash to my spot, slapping hands with Ginger, a short, bouncy redhead, as we trade places and she comes out to rest.

The ball is down by our goal, which makes me nervous. Emily, playing defense, steals the ball and sends it midfield. The Hornets' #3 deadens the ball with the sole of her foot and nudges it forward, then draws her foot back and blasts a shot. Somehow, Courtney, another one of our defenders, gets a foot on it, throwing herself in front of the whizzing ball. She clears it all the way past half field to Latoya. On a breakaway she dribbles as fast as she can, then shoots. The ball bounces off the goalie's shins but pops out right in front of me. My instep connects with the ball, sending it spinning to the side of the goalie, where it nestles into white mesh. The ref's shrill whistle confirms it. Goal!

A rush shoots from my toes to my scalp! I jump up and down and can't contain the smile sweeping over my face.

We're tied. Latoya and Courtney high-five me as we run back to our positions. My roommates' screams echo in my ears.

Head balls, dribbles, passes, shots, turnovers, and missed chances. The game's still tied. We need a goal.

Molly, our goalie, catches one of the Hornets' shots midair and punts the ball upfield. I trap it with my foot and give a quick tap backward to throw off the Hornet guarding me. I regain the ball and push it out in front of me, dribbling as fast as I can. I shoot and feel the ball hit its target as it lands tangled in the net!

Yes!

My heart thumps in time with the clapping hands of the crowd.

We manage to keep the ball away from our goal for the remainder of the game, and the three sharp whistle blasts are like a symphony signaling the end and our win. I'm bubbly all over like I'm filled with Sprite. Since Alex died, I've felt so dang tired, sometimes it feels like I died with him. But right now, in this exhilarating moment, I feel alive.

The thrill of victory sends a surge of adrenaline through my veins. Hannah, Palmer, and Claire all jump up and down as I come off the field. Mama and Daddy stand several feet behind them, immobile like cardboard cutouts. They're so busy missing Alex, they've forgotten to remember me.

"Incredible wedible!" Hannah practically tackles me. "That is so not normal for a freshman to score two goals!"

"We knew you were good." Palmer hugs me, but pulls away and scowls when she feels how sweaty I am. "But you've been holding out, Kat. You should be on the cover of *Sports Illustrated*. Will you agree to an interview?" She holds an imaginary microphone to my mouth.

"No comment," I say, pushing her hand away.

She laughs and almost gallops to my side.

"I'm so proud of you." Claire leans her head on my shoulder.

We're almost next to my folks now.

"Celebrate good times," Hannah sings.

"Your hard work sure is payin' off." Daddy smiles softly. "Where would you like to celebrate, sugar?"

"Schneider's! They have the most amazin' cinnamon rolls!"

"Ooh, sounds so indulgent. I didn't know you had it in you, Kat," Palmer purrs.

"Yeah, I feel a little less guilty about my potato chip fetish," Hannah says. "If Miss Healthy Athlete picks cinnamon rolls, then Schneider's it is."

"We used to get 'em every Sunday mornin'." I smile, remembering the white bakery box perched on our kitchen counter. "Daddy'd sneak out early to the bakery and bring home a box of goodies"

"Guilty." Daddy nods. "I'm a pecan roll kind of guy."

Mama says nothing.

"I always tried to make it downstairs before Alex ate all the cinnamon rolls." I inhale and squeeze my eyes shut. Why did I go there? I thought I wasn't going to go there.

Mama squeaks and breaks the spell of my game.

"So, you and Alex fought over sticky buns?" Hannah asks. "Owen, Sammie, and I always battle for the doughnuts with chocolate frosting on top and the white cream in the middle. You know the kind?"

"I'm a chocolate croissant girl." Palmer shakes her head. "Total weakness."

"*Pain au chocolat*, in French." Claire nods. "I ate them every morning in Paris."

I hear my roommates talking like background noise. They sound normal, happy. I feel hollow, out of place. How can I go from euphoric on the field to flat and achy in a matter of moments? My cleats click against the sidewalk as we reach downtown. The aromas from the row of restaurants—pizza baking, burgers sizzling, cheese melting—make my stomach growl. I'm always famished after games.

"Here we are." Hannah dramatically opens the door to Schneider's.

We order, and I sit with my gooey roll laden with dark brown spice. I sneak a glance at Mama sitting across the table with a bowl of potato soup. Her left eye twitches. She stands and darts to the bathroom.

"Hey, sweetie." Palmer places her hand on my back.

Why does everyone keep touching me? I don't mean to cringe. I know they mean well. But if I feel something, then I'll feel everything, and the pain will be so overpowering I will suffocate under its weight.

"Us girls are taking our treats to go. We'll give you some family time and see you when you get back." Palmer kisses the top of my head.

"Bye," Claire whispers.

"See you later, alligator." Hannah curtsies, and they turn.

I want to stop them, make them stay. I don't think I can face Mama and Daddy without the shield of my roomies, but I guess I have to, at some point.

Daddy sits down with a pecan roll and a cup of coffee. If I bring up Alex, we'll end up talking about *IT* and droning on and on, but if I don't say anything, then this oppressive silence will swallow me whole.

"When is it going to stop?" I demand.

Daddy's eyes mirror the moistness in mine. "I don't know." He shakes his head. "I hoped if we came to your game and went out to celebrate, things would feel normal. Ya know?" Daddy's voice is rich like the frosting on my roll. "We need to keep having things to look forward to. That's what the counselor said. It made sense when he said it, but then it backfires and reminds us of Alex. Everything does." He pounds his fist on the table. "And then none of us verbalizes it and well, shoot, Kat. I don't know what to do." Daddy stretches his enormous hand over mine.

My heart wishes it could crawl out of my chest and hold on to Daddy's heart. It's feeling exactly what he's saying, except what was that part about a counselor?

"Daddy?"

"Yeah." He looks out the window, like he's concentrating on a really far-off place.

"What counselor?"

His eyes shift back to me. "We need to talk about that."

"About what?" The hairs on my arms bristle.

"After Alex, you know." Daddy clears his throat. "I'd say the next day, someone from work recommended a counselor. We went to go see him. Mama and I did. We tried knocking on your door, but you didn't answer." He exhales.

There were lots of knocks and lots of times I ignored them those dark days in Alex's room. I take a sweet, sticky bite of my roll, remembering the buffer of covers I cocooned myself in, closing the world out.

"I don't remember his name, Mama would know." Daddy drums his fingers on the table and looks to the bathroom.

As if on cue, Mama steps out, smoothing her dark hair with her hands. Her green eyes are rimmed in red. She tries to open them brightly, but it's obvious she's been crying.

"I need some fresh air," she says and walks past us.

"What was the name of that counselor we went to see?" Daddy asks her shadow. She doesn't answer. Daddy does for her. "Felix. Yes sir, that's right. He had kind of a big nose and floppy hair."

I try to stifle my reflexive laugh. "Am I going to have to talk to this Felix guy? I hope not."

Daddy laughs quietly. "He asked questions and gave us suggestions on ways to cope. Pretty standard, if you ask me. We weren't all that impressed, so we didn't go back."

Dodged that bullet. If they aren't going back, they can't make me go.

"The two things he said that did make sense were that we should try to stay consistent with our routines—work, school, activities, meals, and the like—and that we should plan something to look forward to."

I eat my frosting in little flakes. Next, I pick up the naked pastry and unspiral it, starting on the end and eating it along like a string, saving the gooey center for last. It's sweeter and softer and spicier than any cinnamon roll, ever. Maybe it's because I realize we only have a finite number of cinnamon rolls in life, so I better enjoy it while I can. Is that incredibly selfish? I should be focused on Alex, right? Still, I can't help licking my lips.

"Kat?"

"Mm-hm," I mumble.

"Mama and I, well, we didn't really need to see the counselor again. We felt once was enough, for us."

Clearly. They're so well adjusted now.

"But we thought it might help you, you know, if you wanted to talk to someone, not Felix." Daddy wiggles his jaw from side to side, like he's trying to loosen it.

I stop mid-bite. "Why would I do that?" I think of Claire and her counselor. Did she say her name was Amy?

"Well, you could—" Daddy clears his throat again. "You know, talk to them about how you feel."

"How do you feel, Daddy?" I shoot back.

He averts my eyes and gazes into the dark pools of his coffee.

"How does Mama feel?" I look out the window. "Where'd she go, anyway?"

Daddy shakes his head, staring into his mug. "She does that a lot these days," he whispers.

Daddy might as well have disappeared with her, he's so far removed. Maybe Mama's down there swimming in his cup. She's physically gone, and he's mentally gone.

I explode. Pushing myself away from the table I stand and say, "Why did y'all come? It's obvious y'all don't want to be here."

I turn my back to the shell of my daddy, praying he'll stop me, that he'll apologize or at least call out. But he doesn't. And I walk out the door.

CHAPTER TWENTY-NINE – HANNAH

"SURPRISE!" I SQUEAL WHEN MY friends are finally back from class and gathered in the main room of our two-room suite. I had early classes this morning and have been decorating ever since.

"Pumpkins." Claire smiles. "Soooo cute. Where did you get them?"

My heart skips in excitement. I spent a long time picking them out—not too tiny, but not so big that I couldn't carry them back to our room. I wanted ones with smooth surfaces so we could decorate them, and they needed to be bright orange—nice and cheery.

"At that little market on campus where you can buy Tylenol and Gatorade and stuff. They had pumpkins. I couldn't resist." I bounce on my toes. "I thought we could decorate them tonight."

"So fun," Palmer says. "Can we use paint pens? I have a whole bag of them. I think I'm going to make mine into a cat."

"What?" Kat jerks her head.

I so hoped a little festivity would make her smile.

"Oh, silly, I said I'd make my pumpkin into a cat, as in meow, not as in you, Kat." Palmer grins and shakes her head at Kat, who's drumming her DayGlo orange thumbs on the back of the futon.

"Cool." Kat seems to snap out of her haze. "I'll make mine into a soccer ball." The tiniest hint of a grin sneaks across her face.

"Yay." My heart flutters. It's working. "How about you, Claire?"

"I don't know yet." She tosses her hair over one shoulder examining the pumpkins. "I need to think about it. It looks great in here, Hannah." She bats an orange streamer from the ceiling. "You rule."

"Thanks." I shrug.

"The paper bats are adorable." Palmer nods at the construction paper critters I've hung from the ceiling and taped to the windows. "Purple, of course. Only you, Han, would make purple bats."

"What?" I ask in mock defense. "Purple is spooky. Sort of."

"Hmm." Palmer winks. "It makes the orange stand out better, but it is *your* favorite color."

"Guilty." I laugh. "Okay, this is so fun. Everyone pick a pumpkin. And I grabbed these scrumptious-looking pumpkin muffins at the dining hall." I spring over to the table where I've displayed four muffins on cute ghost napkins I also grabbed from the dining hall.

I throw my hands to my quickly reddening face. "Oh my gosh. You don't think it was stealing, do you? Taking them from the dining hall?"

"No." Palmer shakes her head and kisses my cheek. "Stop hyperventilating. Have you seen some of those football players? I bet that one guy—I honestly think his friends call him Huge Guy—ate a dozen muffins at breakfast, at least, maybe two dozen. We all have dining hall passes. We could have each gotten one." Palmer slides her arm down on the small of my back and rubs it.

My insides shake and little beads of sweat form along my hairline. What if it was stealing? I blow my bangs out of my eyes. Why do I let myself get so worked up?

"I grab stuff from the dining hall all the time. I barely ever have time to sit down and eat. It doesn't matter if you eat it here or there." Claire curls onto the futon. "It was sweet of you. And I'm starving." She grabs a muffin and bites into it, frosting sticking to her lips like a mustache. "Yummy. You should have gotten more."

Thanks, God, for roommates who don't judge me, even when I judge myself.

My shoulders sink another inch and my jaw unclenches. Just like every time I turn something over to God, I feel better.

"I'm gonna shower." Kat nods toward our bathroom. She's wearing running tights, a thick sweatshirt, a knit cap, and Nike gloves.

I nod like crazy. "I am so sorry. I forgot you came straight from practice."

"Not a problem. I was all sweaty, and then my sweat kind of froze on me on the way home. I'll be out in a few."

Palmer spreads a newspaper on the floor, the pages crinkling as she unfolds them.

I grab a muffin. "Mmm. I love that spicy cinnamon thingy these have going on."

"Delish! I'll have to make some over Thanksgiving." Palmer wipes a crumb from the corner of her mouth. "Hey, guys?" she asks, still sitting on the floor but leaning back against the futon where Claire's toes dangle.

"Yeah," Claire and I say in unison. Claire tips her head forward so her hair covers Palmer's face.

Palmer giggles, brushing Claire's curls away. "Do you think I'm fat?"

"What?" I ask.

Claire shakes her head and scrunches her nose.

"No. Seriously." Palmer squares her shoulders. "I want you to be honest. Mom hinted I've put on some weight, and maybe I have, but it's so hard to resist something like this." She holds up the muffin. "But I would despise myself if I gained the dreaded freshman fifteen."

"You are so beautiful," Claire says.

If anyone ever told me I was beautiful the way Claire just did, I'd be convinced I was a princess. I get that subtle stab of jealousy I often experience being perfect Palmer's best friend, but Claire's right.

I nod. "You're, like, twenty pounds lighter than I am, so I'm really in trouble if you're fat."

"That is so not true!" Palmer swats me with a pillow. "You are perfect, Han."

"Hmm." I raise an eyebrow. "If I'm so perfect, then why can't I get a single guy to like me?"

"You can have one of mine," Kat says, stepping back into the room in shorts and a T-shirt, kneading her wet hair with a towel.

"Thanks for rubbing it in." I laugh. "So who's winning? Tony or Nicholas?"

"Ugh." Kat plops next to Claire. She smells fresh like lemons and suds. "Guys are the last thing I wanna think about. Nicholas is a doll. He was so good to me at the funeral." Her voice clogs up. She sniffs and shakes her head. "But then I saw Tony in the weight room this mornin', and he didn't say one thing about Alex or the funeral or ask me how I'm doin', 'cause I don't think he even knows about it. And it was nice, ya know, to just talk soccer and not have to go *there*." Kat's face contorts.

Crap. I wanted tonight to be all about fun and getting everyone's mind off everything.

"We love you, Kat." Claire snuggles into Kat's shoulder.

"True, true," I say, sliding into the hug.

"Make room for me!" Palmer squashes herself in sideways.

We teeter and wobble and sway, then totter, thudding onto the floor in one convoluted heap of roommates and pumpkins.

"Is that somebody's elbow?" Kat groans.

"I think it's a pumpkin stem."

And we all laugh uncontrollably as we try to untangle our limbs without smashing the pumpkins.

CHAPTER THIRTY – KAT

IT DOESN'T MATTER THAT I'M tired or disoriented or that I feel I might literally break into hundreds of little pieces. Between leaving for Spain and soccer season ending, I wake up just knowing this is going to be one of my harder days, but I need to stay in condition. I need stamina, more stamina than anyone else looking for the spot of starting midfielder on the Varsity team for next year.

I roll out of bed and slide on running tights, footies, and a long-sleeved tee. I dive into my coziest sweatshirt, my gray Clarkston one with the hood. Mama and Daddy must still be asleep. The house is deathly quiet.

I hate that word.

It does feel like death around here, though—like death has seeped into every crevice of our lives, even our sleeping, even the brick and mortar of our house. I flip on the lights and dig around the laundry room for my shoes. I pull a baseball cap off the hook. It's Alex's OSU cap.

The pain of missing him cuts my throat and rides up across my tongue like a circular saw. Tears burn my skin as they slide down my face. I punch the garage door opener and am assaulted by the pounding of a downpour.

I knew today was going to be a hard one.

I stretch in the garage, wobbly, unsteady, still half-asleep. I step onto the driveway where I'm instantly pelted with cold, wet drops. I pull Alex's hat down farther, pulling him closer to me, barely allowing room for my eyes to peek out.

There is no daylight because of the hour, because of the clouds. Around me there is darkness, and I am lost in it. Most mornings I'm up early for practice just in time to watch the sun creep over the horizon, but the sun stayed in bed today. I don't blame it. I'd love to crawl under my covers and stay there until it's my turn to die, in hopes of seeing Alex again. Will I see him when I die? Is that what heaven's like? What if I never see him again?

My feet move automatically. Left, right, left, right.

Sploosh, splash, whoosh.

There are no streetlights in our neighborhood to guide me. I run forward, only by memory of where the street should be, guided by shadows. My left foot lands on something that could be a pinecone or a dead mouse. I cringe but keep running. Four steps, five steps. My right foot lands smack into a puddle.

I feel helpless out here. I could slip. I could stumble. I could get hit by a car. I feel like I'm drowning. The rain engulfs me. It sloshes in my shoes and drips into my ears. My sweatshirt clings to my body.

God, help me.

I wonder if my prayer is for this run or for my life. I feel like I'm being pulled down, down, under water, but yet I keep running, one foot after the other, left, right, left, right. Maybe the demons won't be fast enough to chase me to Spain. Maybe if I run fast enough, I can outrun them. My passport came in the mail last week. My suitcase's been packed and sitting on the counter of my dorm room for days. Hannah, Palmer, and I rode back to Columbus together yesterday afternoon.

As I make the final turn toward our house, I realize the rain has slowed to a damp drizzle. In the sky high and to the right, clouds part allowing a streak of white light to sneak through the gap. It is just one beam of light, one ray of hope, but it is something.

That something is my motivation to get through. At least through today.

AN HOUR LATER, SHOWERED AND dressed, Daddy's voice beckons, "Ready, Kat?"

"Ready!"

I grab my suitcase, check my purse for my passport, sling it across my shoulder, and bound down the stairs.

Mama's nowhere to be seen. We're leaving for a five-day trip on the other side of the world, and she's not even here to say good-bye. She should be coming with us. I've secretly hoped all week she'd change her mind. Somehow, I thought, if we could all experience Barcelona together, we could learn to get through everything together. I mean, this trip is just our solution to avoid Thanksgiving, but we'll get back and then we'll need to figure out how we're going to get through Christmas and Alex's birthday and every day in between and after.

"I'll put your suitcase in the trunk." Daddy grabs my bag.

"Thanks, Daddy." Glancing around the kitchen, I sense something's about to change—that I'll go to Barcelona and come back to something different. Maybe that's putting too much pressure on this trip. Maybe I have too high expectations, but I can't stand thinking of us living like zombies forever.

I don't want to come back and have Alex's chair gone from the table or find Mama's hung some plaque for him over the front door. I don't want anything to look different, because there's an odd comfort to home, but I want everything to *feel* different. Different from this. I tap my ring on the leather trim of my purse and climb into the car.

At the airport we're corralled like cattle into sanctioned lines at security. We set our carry-on bags on the conveyer belt. I slide off my comfy TOMS shoes and place them in a plastic tub along with my phone.

"Isn't it weird they make us take off our shoes?" I whisper to Daddy, suddenly paranoid I look suspicious to the guards in dark uniforms.

"It's just a precaution. No one can hide anything in their shoes if they have to take them off."

"Could someone hide somethin' in their shoes?" My mind races.

"Not likely, since everyone knows they're going have to put their shoes through the scanner. Remember one of those al Qaeda guys tried to ignite a liquid bomb in his shoes, way back in 2001, I think. You're probably too young to remember."

I blink. If terrorists could sneak bombs in their shoes, where else could they sneak something explosive? Would anyone want to terrorize a flight to Barcelona? All this time I've been romanticizing about cafés and cobblestone streets. Why hadn't I considered the whole terrorist thing? I never used to worry about dying, but now it seems like everywhere I go is filled with danger. I used to feel invulnerable, but now I ooze vulnerability. And I hate it.

"Is this safe, Daddy?" I grab his arm.

"It's safe, sugar. Thousands of people go through there every day. It's just a glorified metal detector." Daddy nods toward the metal arch.

"I meant flying to another country, not going through the metal detector."

"Miss." A large woman with a severe expression and a hideous hairnet motions for me to enter the arch.

I guardedly walk toward her, reminding myself never to take a job where hairnets are required, and stand obediently in the scanner until she waves me forward.

I gather my things from the conveyer belt, which smells like tires, and reassemble myself. When Daddy joins me, I demand, "Are you sure our flight's safe?"

"Darlin', security is tight as a drum these days. We're safer here than we are about anywhere. Relax. That's what this trip is for. How about we grab a coffee before our flight? That sounds good now, doesn't it?"

Out of the corner of my eye I spy a guard frisking a man sporting a navy suit. What's behind those sunglasses? Is he too pale?

Behind him, two twenty-something girls whisper and fumble through ginormous purses, fiddling with excessive amounts of zippers on their high-heeled boots. What's in their bags? Is all their fuss a distraction?

I reach to tug on Daddy's sleeve, to ask him what he thinks, but he's ten steps ahead.

"Daddy!" I trot forward. I knew I shouldn't have stayed up and watched the newest Jason Bourne movie with Palmer the other night. It's totally feeding my frenzy.

At the coffee counter I order a chai latte. The warmth of the steaming tea through the cup feels good in my hands. I inhale the rich scents of cardamom and

cinnamon and sip the sweet, frothy drink, thinking first of
Nicholas and our walk, then of Alex in heaven,
surrounded by the smells from my cup and the warmth of
my drink.

CHAPTER THIRTY-ONE – PALMER

I CRACK EGGS ONE AT a time in the giant glass bowl. I add vanilla, sniffing the delicious fragrance before putting the cap back on. I pour thick Karo syrup, watching it slowly glug into the bowl, and lastly, I kerplunk a bag of chopped pecans into the mixture.

Whizzirrizzzirr.

The blades on the beaters spin round and round, incorporating the sweet, sticky mass into the perfect filling for my pecan pie. When the filling's well blended, I pour it into my piecrust, cover it with foil, and slide it into the warm oven, setting the timer as soon as I secure the door.

Turning to my iHome, I fiddle to find a good play list. Humming along with Jamie Grace, I pull out pumpkin, cinnamon, sweetened condensed milk, nutmeg, and cloves for my next delicacy.

"It smells delish in here," Tia says, plopping herself onto one of the barstools. "Whatcha making?"

"I've got a pecan pie baking, and I'm getting ready to start on the pumpkin." I grin, waving a measuring spoon at my sister.

"Yum! Pumpkin's my fav. Can I make the whipped cream?"

"You can whip the cream Thursday morning. It has to be fresh, but you can help me make the pie now."

"I'm in." Tia jumps up and digs through a drawer. "Apron?" She holds one out with a pilgrim on it.

"Oh my gosh. Where did Mom get this?"

"Duh. Pottery Barn." Tia laughs, wrapping an apron that looks like an Indian outfit around her. "Aren't they great? I've been waiting for you to get home so we could wear them. We so need to get our picture taken. Mom!"

"What?" Mom clips into the kitchen, decked out for the day in silk slacks, a tweed blazer, and plum lipstick. "Well, you didn't waste any time diving back into the kitchen, Palmer. Don't you two look adorable?" She laughs.

"I miss having a kitchen." I exhale, running my hand along the controls of the stove. "I can't cook anything in our dorm room."

"You've always loved to cook." Mom shakes her head. "That's your father's side. The Italian in you. It will totally win the right man's heart someday. Just be careful." She eyes my waistline, which I immediately suck in.

"Take our picture, pretty please?" Tia begs.

"Sure."

I pull my phone from my pocket and hand it to her.

"All right, girls, on three. One. Two. Three."

Click.

"Very nice. You two could be in the catalog." Mom looks at the screen, checking her photography skills.

"Take another one, okay?" Tia asks. "This one's crazy."

"All right." Mom sighs. "One. Two. Three."

I stick out my tongue and Tia puffs out her cheeks. We all three burst into giggles.

"I have a nail appointment," Mom says, handing me back my phone. "I'll be back in a bit."

"Have fun."

"Okay," Tia and I chorus.

As Mom's flats *click, clack* out of the kitchen, Tia and I huddle over my phone examining the pictures. "These are awesome," Tia says, then she lowers her voice, "I missed you, Palm."

"I missed you too, sweet sissy." I hug her sideways. "Hey, why don't we get the pie in the oven, then run to Starbucks and get Pumpkin Spiced Lattes? My treat."

"Really?" Tia's dark eyes widen.

"Um-hm." I nod. "The pumpkin needs to bake for over half an hour, which gives us plenty of time to get there and back."

Once our next pie is nestled in the oven, we pile into my Mini Cooper. After the short drive, Tia pulls into a parking spot in front of Starbucks.

"Thanks for driving." I grin as we walk through the chilly parking lot toward the door.

"Thanks for letting me."

I tug on the door, warmed by the heated air and thick aroma of coffee. "Mmm. I love this place." I smile.

One second later my smile evaporates.

By the window sits Keegan with Carly Peterson, a senior in high school. Cups are on the table in front of them, but neither of them are drinking their coffee. Carly's giggling uncontrollably and leaning so close to Keegan I think her chest, which is popping out of her extreme V-neck sweater, is bumping Keegan's arm. He grins at her like she's a Christmas present he can't wait to unwrap.

"Gag me with a coffee cup." Tia elbows me. "She really should wear a cami under that."

It feels like there is a coffee pot lodged in my throat and the hot contents burn my insides. Speechless, I step into line.

CHAPTER THIRTY-TWO – KAT

OUT THE WINDOW THE DARK landmass below gets closer and closer. My window feels warm to the touch. People always speak of heaven as being in the sky. Where is it?

Am I passing through?

All I see is endless blue strewn with wisps of white. Do I need to go higher? Is heaven visible if you're still alive? If I look hard enough, will I see Alex out my window? He must be up here, right? Tears prick the corners of my bleary eyes.

Daddy shuts down his laptop, puts his hand on my arm, and asks, "Did you get some sleep?"

I nod and try to clear my throat. "You?"

"I slept some. You ready for this?" Daddy's eyes flash a glint of gold. That glow means somewhere in him he still believes it's okay to have happiness.

Am I ready? Ready to be away from everything and everyone I know—to immerse myself in a land where the language trills and rolls and the culture is so warm, it just might melt my fears, and where the entire population is obsessed by soccer?

"So ready!"

We bounce on the ground, zooming down the tarmac at full speed.

"You're going to love it here." Daddy winks.

"I know," I eek. Somewhere in my heart, I know.

Exiting the Jetway, rapid-fire Spanish fills my ears. "Wow!" I say, stopping to take in the bright lights, shiny floors, and shops with neon signs. If it weren't for the Spanish, I could be back in the Columbus airport, or any airport for that matter.

We maneuver to ground transportation where forty or so drivers hold signs with printed names. The flood of Spanish sounds like a violin concerto, not words, but lovely notes rising up and down, flying off tongues like music off a bow.

Daddy sees our name. Pointing, he says, "Wiley, that's us."

Our cab is actually a van. We lurch into traffic. Everything's chaotic and crowded. There are cars and people and buses and bicycles and more people everywhere.

I snap photos with my phone of colorful awnings and small wrought-ironed balconies poking out of narrow streets. My eyes can't drink in enough details. I want to remember it all. Everything is so different from home— nothing here to remind me of Alex, of what happened.

As we weave through the streets, I gaze at the people—some with skin the color of gingerbread, others pale white with black hair, and a few even wear turbans. Some look like they could go to Clarkston with me, meandering down streets in boots and scarves. Men congregate on street corners, gesturing. Children with hands shoved in their pockets follow behind their mothers.

At our hotel, the St. Agusti, we settle in our room. I place my teddy bear, Cooper, who still travels with me everywhere, on the cream-colored bedspread of the bed I've claimed as mine.

Daddy rubs his jaw. "We could take a rest. I know neither of us slept much on that plane, but if you're ready, I think it'd be nice to go exploring."

My weariness disappears as excitement rises in my chest, like right before a game—an eagerness to get started. "Let's go!"

"Sounds good." Daddy's eyes shine.

After endless hours of being confined in a plane, I feel like a cheetah escaping her cage at the zoo. My muscles stretch and flex with each step. We traipse down a cobblestone street that runs smack into Las Ramblas, the heart of Barcelona, a long wide street with a median for pedestrians jammed with street performers, musicians, and vendors. Daddy and I walk, listening to birdcalls and laughter, taking in bright flowers and the smell of baking bread. There's so much to see I keep jerking my head back and forth, afraid I'll miss something. I could lose myself in this city. Maybe I can lose my memories here too.

"Let's get ourselves somethin' to drink." Daddy's drawl has been slowly thickening since we boarded the plane. I like the smooth, relaxed tone.

"This coffee shop's cute," I say, grabbing the crook of Daddy's arm.

We sit at a small circular table out front of the shop. We sit for a long time before a man in a white apron serves us strong, steaming espresso in tiny white cups, but I'm in no hurry. Daddy and I sit and listen to the clattering of cups and the buzz of Vespas zooming through the streets.

"It's so weird that it's mornin' here." I shake my head. "We flew forever and a day, and when we get here, these people are just headin' off to school or work or whatever."

"Amazin', isn't it?" Daddy nods and leans back in his chair.

We watch a mime dressed in gold, like an angel, wings and all, standing as still as a statue as passersby stop and drop coins in her cup. We sip our espresso, too strong to slurp, and absorb our surroundings.

"This is good." Daddy sets down his cup.

"The espresso?" I ask, thinking how different it tastes from what we drink at home.

"Sure, the coffee's good." Daddy rocks slowly back and forth in his chair. "Comin' here's good too. I'm glad you came with me, Kat."

"Me too." I smile and take his outreached hand.

CHAPTER THIRTY-THREE – CLAIRE

"YOU AND YOUR MOM LOOK so much alike." Aunt Denise smiles, but I cringe. I see something behind her eyes. Suddenly the scuffs on my favorite cowboy boots seem deeper and my consignment shop denim jacket seems less vintage and more used.

"Hi, Aunt Denise." I squeeze her, breathing in her ritzy perfume. "It's really nice of you to invite Mom and me for Thanksgiving. Thanks."

"Of course." Aunt Denise waves her hand. "What's family for? I couldn't imagine the two of you eating frozen dinners, or whatever your mom serves you, in that rinky-dink apartment for a holiday. This will be so much better. Don't you think?"

We wouldn't be eating frozen dinners, probably Chinese, but Aunt Denise will throw a magnificent feast complete with sweet potatoes and cranberries. And I have to admit the wood floors and high ceilings of her place are reminiscent of a luxury hotel. That's what I'll do. I'll pretend I'm a famous dancer on holiday at a secretly tucked-away luxury hotel in Michigan. Way better than worrying about what Aunt Denise thinks about me.

"You're such a great cook. It'll be great." I sniff. "In fact, something smells delicious."

"Oh, that? Just a pear and cherry cobbler I'm baking. I'll serve it with ice cream and decaf when your mom arrives. A little welcome gathering."

My mouth waters. "Yum!" I look around. "She's not here yet?"

Typical. I rode a bus for six hours and still beat Mom.

"Not quite." Aunt Denise bites her lip. "But I'm sure she'll be here soon. And Megan can't wait to see you. She's in her room. Why don't you take your things up and say hello. I have you in the guest room right next to hers." She glances at my backpack. "Where are the rest of your things, honey?"

"This is it." I tug my sunglasses off my head where they rested like a headband.

"Oh. Okay." Aunt Denise looks behind me as if she's expecting my backpack to expand into a steamer trunk. "Well, you remember where her room is? Up the stairs and *third* door on the right?"

"I remember." Does Mom even have three doors in her new apartment? Maybe coming here for Thanksgiving wasn't such a bad idea after all. Maybe if I treat it as a retreat, it will be one.

I head up the stairs and walk past my cousin's closed door. She's always been nice enough, but I am not her favorite person. I don't really fit the criteria Megan has for friends:

1. Rich
2. Gorgeous
3. Knows they're rich and gorgeous

It's never bothered me, though. Not much. I only see her in small doses.

The door to my room is open, revealing a vase with yellow roses on the nightstand next to the bed covered with a thick, moss-colored quilt. I toss my backpack on the floor and crash on the bed for a second. Ahh. This is going to be way better than sharing a bed with Mom in the midst of her packing boxes. Why was I so worked up about it? "Fancy bedroom all to myself" will definitely make my thankful list.

I use the bathroom, wash my face, brush my teeth, and spritz some perfume, trying to get rid of the Greyhound grunge. Maybe I could live *here* this summer? They certainly have room. If I got a job at a dance studio, I could pay for some things and stay out of everyone's way. My mind swirls around the potential.

I tap on Megan's closed door. "Hey, Meg, it's me, Claire."

I hear her swear and then there's some hurried rustling. A minute later Megan opens the door. Her long blond hair practically shimmers. It's so shiny and perfectly ironed straight. "Hey." She smiles and opens her pale blue eyes really wide. She wobbles a bit as she lets me in her room. It smells like heavy incense and something else, something sweet and heady I can't put my finger on.

"Wow. Like you came all the way from Ohio for Thanksgiving," Megan says slowly and sinks into an armchair.

I sprawl across her ginormous king-sized bed. "Yeah. The bus ride was pretty long." I untie the scarf from my neck and wrap it around my head like a headband. "So what's U of M like?" I ask, spitting out the topics of conversation I'd planned ahead of time. "Is it big?"

"It is, like, the most hugest place I've ever been." Megan's words sound sluggish. "But I've made a million and ten friends. My dorm is so cool. And my R.A. is, like, never around, so we can do whatever we want."

Losing the chill of the bus ride thanks to the warmth of their heater, I slide off my jacket.

"Great shirt." Megan comes over and grabs a section of my sleeve between her thumb and pointer finger, rubbing the fabric. "Like, where did you get it?"

"I don't know. A little shop on campus." I don't mention it was in the final sale bin for $4.99 because it had missing buttons, or that Hannah sewed some cool black velvet ones on for me.

"What do you mean? Like, who designed it?"

"I have no idea." I laugh. "Palmer, one of my roommates, would know, I'm sure. She's very into fashion. You two might get along."

"Is she rich?" Megan raises her eyebrows.

"I guess." I sniff again, but the pear cobbler and incense muffle the other smell, the thicker one. What is that? "She has all kinds of gorgeous clothes. Palmer has boots that cost more than all of my clothes put together." I laugh. "And I went to her house once. It was palatial. So, yeah, I guess."

Megan leans forward, hanging on my every word. I don't want to use Palmer to impress Megan. I never think of Palm like that. I add, "But she's not snooty at all. She doesn't talk about her money. She's super generous."

"Hmm." Megan raises her eyebrows as if trying to comprehend why someone wouldn't flaunt their money.

Megan crawls behind me and tugs on the collar of my shirt to check the label.

"Sabrina. Never heard of it. Cute, though, in an indie sort of way."

"Thanks." I wriggle my shoulders when she lets go of my collar, her breath laden with that scent. "Pot. That's what I smell," I say, looking at her, not trying to accuse, just relieved I figured it out. "The skate punks smoke it outside our apartment all the time. That's why I recognized it. You smoke pot?"

"*Shusssshh!*" Megan puts her hand over my mouth and then falls back next to me on her bed laughing.

CHAPTER THIRTY-FOUR – PALMER

TIA COVERS MY MOUTH WITH her hand as we walk back to the car.

Once the doors are closed, she ungags me, and I scream, "What a jerk! He was trying to console me at Alex's funeral after telling me I looked hot, and now he's got his face down Carly's shirt."

"I used to think you had it all, dating Keegan." Tia backs out of our parking spot. "But he's really a jerk, huh? What got into him, anyway?"

I sniffle, trying to catch my tears with a Kleenex before they smear my mascara. "Sex."

"Get out!" Tia slams her hand on the steering wheel. "You and Keegan had sex! Holy cow, Palm. When? What was it like? Did it hurt? I'm so scared it's going to hurt."

Am I really having this conversation with my little sister? I look over and can't believe how old Tia looks. Since she got her braces off her teeth look perfect. And our hairdresser, Patrick, does an amazing job with her hair. He gave her these fab little spiky layered ends to her long, thick mane. Let's face it. We both got lucky with Dad's Italian genes, olive skin, dark eyes, full lips. She could totally fit in on campus.

"No!" I spurt. "I didn't. We didn't. I mean, he wants to, I guess he wanted to, now he might actually be doing it with Carly. Oh, Tia, what if he's having sex with Carly because I wouldn't sleep with him?"

"Then he's a creep, is what." Tia puts on the turn signal. "So you didn't. Dang. I need the inside scoop."

"You're not thinking about having sex, are you?" I ask, my insides cold and hard and clanging.

"No. Of course not." Tia rolls her eyes, but I'm not convinced. "It's just, Jonathon, translation dreamy, invited me to the Christmas dance, and he is so hot. Oh, never mind." She shakes her head.

"You cannot sleep with him." I put my hand on her arm. "Listen. I know it's hard. Oh my gosh, there were, like, ten times I almost did it with Keegan."

"Really?"

"No joke." I remember my latte and sip creamy pumpkin sweetness. "Okay, this is so good."

Tia takes a sip of hers too. "Delish. It's hard to stop drinking it." She sips again.

"Right. So that's exactly what sex is like."

"I thought you said you didn't!" Tia squeals.

"I didn't." I laugh. "I mean, Keegan and I would be making out, and getting close, and everything would feel so good, like this latte, but way more intense." I raise my eyebrows. "And I knew I should stop. Just like I know I should *sip* my coffee, not chug it, because it would burn my throat, plus it would be all gone." I peek in the tiny hole on top where I've left lipstick stains, making sure there's still plenty. "It makes me squirmy even talking about it. It was like, I craved him, but that was so wrong, Tia. You can't even let it get that far, because the further you go, the harder it is to stop."

"Why is it so wrong? I mean, besides the Bible and all that."

"Okay, one, because the Bible's a big deal. And two, because of what we just saw. Right?"

Tia tilts her head and bites her lip. "I don't follow."

"I thought Keegan and I were meant for each other. We'd even picked out names for our kids, for crying out loud!"

"Was one of them Tia?" She bats her eyelashes.

"Uh. No. But I thought we were a match made in heaven, that we'd for sure get married, so I half thought about sleeping with him, because we were in love. But something, a little voice inside me, and I know it sounds dorky, but I really think it was God, said not to. The voice told me to stop. Every time it told me to stop, I could somehow pull out of the intensity of it all and say no. The voice gave me strength."

"That's really cool, Palm." Tia looks at me, her voice soft.

"Yeah." I nod, a bit amazed myself that God was there all along, helping me be strong. "It is cool. And now I see why it was so important. Why God helped me again and again say no." I take another sip of coffee, letting the cinnamon and cream roll around on my tongue. "Keegan's already on to someone else. He wasn't 'the one.' Even though I thought he was. I really thought he was." My voice clogs and the tears return.

"What you did is really awesome." Tia punches my car into park on our driveway and grabs my hand.

I nod, afraid if I speak the tears will explode.

Tia hands me another Kleenex. "Hey. You did the right thing. You are so beautiful and so way amazing. His loss, sweetie."

"Right." I snort and nod, loving Tia for loving me so much. "Here's the deal, T. Let's make a pact, you and me, that we'll save ourselves for our wedding nights.

That way, we'll never give ourselves away to the wrong guy."

"Pinkie promise." Tia holds up her pinkie in a crook. I hold up mine and we shake on it.

BACK IN MY ROOM I grab my journal.

Things I'm thankful for . . . I doodle in thick script on the top of a fresh page. I bite the end of my pen.

1. Pact with Tia
2. Pumpkin lattes
3. Movie night and brownies with roomies before we headed home

Thunder pounces on my bed, her purr motor on full throttle. "Hi, Thunderkinz. I know. I missed you too, sweetie."

4. Thunder, who loves me unconditionally

I think of Keegan, who apparently doesn't love me at all.

5. God giving me strength to say no to Keegan. (Wow, at the time I didn't know what a gift that was. THANK YOU, GOD!)
6. Michael, the editor, who is smarter, more mature, and has a better future ahead of him than Keegan. Although his eyes aren't as intoxicating, and I don't really know about his smell, because at the library everything smells like library, and then at Mr. Mustard's, where we ate lunch, everything smells like grease.
7. The chance to figure out Michael's smell

"Palmer, I have your boots." Tia tromps into my room holding my beloved Tory Burch black leather boots with the shiny T on the sides.

8. Boots—totally stylin' boots

CHAPTER THIRTY-FIVE – KAT

"YOU BE CAREFUL TODAY. YOU'LL be all right, won't you?" Daddy's eyes cloud over for a moment. "By yourself."

"I'll be fine." I lean over and touch my toes. I stand and shake my arms and legs. I'm stretching like I do every morning, but I'm also trying to shake off Daddy's inference. I know he's thinking of Alex, that he could lose me too. I know because I think like that all the time.

"I have my phone. You said you set it up for here, right? I have my map. And you'll be back by four. Right?" My words are meant to convince both of us.

"Mm-hm, that's all right, phone, map, four." Daddy slides one hotel key in his pocket and hands me the other one along with some Euros. "Be safe, sugar. Be smart." Daddy's voice catches in his throat, and he looks down at his shoes. "And have yourself some fun."

"You too." I hug him. "You be safe and smart. We need each other."

Daddy gives me a tight squeeze, coughs, and steps back. "All right, then. Four o'clock. Why don't you text me every hour, just to check in. And call me if you need me. Oh, and keep track of your bag. Wear your money belt."

I roll my eyes. "Dorky."

"No one sees it, Kat. You wear it under your sweatshirt. Barcelona is notorious for pickpockets."

"Got it. Stay clear of Oliver Twist."

"Enjoy yourself, now." He laughs and walks out the door.

I slide on running clothes and gym shoes. I tuck my room key and some Euros in the little inside zipper pocket of my running pants and grab my phone and earbuds. Loaded up to Brad Paisley's crooning, I'm ready to run.

On the street I'm confronted with the crush of humanity. The sidewalks are crammed. I dodge a man in a black trench coat, only to bump into an Asian woman in front of him. I apologize and search for an opening. There's a bit of room in the middle of the sidewalk, but after five steps, I'm at an intersection with a red light. When the light changes, I cross the street and am bombarded by a shabby-looking guy thrusting a balloon in my face. Everywhere I look is jammed. I shake my head and laugh. Looks like running is out of the question.

Plan B.

I U-turn back to the hotel and swap my running clothes for climbing clothes, stuff my tan money belt with money and my passport, and toss my soccer ball, although prospects of finding enough open space to kick look slim, my aluminum water bottle, and the hotel notepad and pen in my string bag.

"*Perdon?*" I ask the clerk on my way out.

"*Si, señorita?*"

I try to form the sentence in Spanish, but the English pops out instead. "Do you have any information on Montserrat?"

"Yes, of course." He hands me a slick brochure depicting a yellow building, nestled in fairy-tale-looking mountains. "It is very easy, yes. You take the train for about ninety minutes. And," he pauses, pointing out the photos in the brochure, "you spend a few hours, then take the train back to Barcelona." His tongue rolls around the *c* in Barcelona. "You might get something to eat to take with you."

"*Gracias*." I smile, sliding the brochure into my string bag. In minutes I'm walking along Las Ramblas again. The air is thick with cigarette smoke and body odor and exhaust fumes, but it is also full of spicy perfume and fresh flowers and delicious aromas floating from stands and cafés.

There are people and more people everywhere I look. I get bumped twice, jumping both times. Daddy's warning of pickpockets buzzes in my ears. I tap my belt with my valuables.

I spy Café Zurich's yellow awning, where Daddy and I got coffee yesterday. Ducking inside, I'm overtaken by the sweet, rich scent of chocolate mingled with bold espresso. My stomach grumbles. I settle into a wooden chair away from the chaos of the street and order churros and a *chocolata a la tassa*, because, well, it is vacation, and even though I can't run, I'm definitely hiking on Montserrat.

While I wait for the server to bring my order, I pull out the notepad from the hotel. I print:
THANKFUL LIST
I start to write the date, but can't. In one instant the excitement of my adventure is stolen, and I'm filled with emptiness—as blank and stark as the page in front of me. I drum my pinky ring on the paper, trying to revive my

eagerness to seize the day. But it's no use. My heart feels hollow. Today is the day before Thanksgiving, and I miss Alex. I bite my lip and rock my weight forward and back.

"*Señorita.*" My server clanks down a plate piled with ridged strips of fried dough that look like they came out of a Play-Doh machine and a small white cup on a saucer.

"*Gracias,*" I say.

The hot chocolate tastes like someone melted an entire Hershey bar directly into my cup. Something for the list.

1. CHOCOLATA A LA TASSA

Imitating the other customers, I dip the end of a churro in my hot chocolate. A dark brown drop dribbles on my notepad. It's so good, like a cinnamon doughnut with chocolate frosting. The spots will be proof to my roomies that I did my homework in Spain. Proof to me that there is something to be thankful for.

I snap a picture of my food and post it on Instagram. More proof.

I wish I could send it to Alex. He would love this place.

It feels like I didn't swallow my last bite of churro, like there's a lump of fried dough in my throat. He would love it here. Why can't he be here? This was supposed to be *our* trip. Maybe that's why I'm suddenly such a mess.

My stomach twitters like when Daddy used to spin Alex and me on the tire swing hanging from the giant oak in one of the first backyards I remember, the one in Alabama. If Alex were here, this would be an adventure, the two of us exploring Barca. Together.

Without him it seems too big for me to tackle.

This is not who I want to be.

I hate being weak and squiggly. Just because something happened to Alex doesn't mean I have to fall apart. Does it? I want to be strong and confident again.

You are strong! I hear in the recesses of my brain.

I used to be. I nod. *But that was because of Alex.*

Really? Or is that just what you're telling yourself?

I pay my bill and pull out my map, trying to process the prodding in my soul.

Am I still brave? A solo hike in the hills should be a good test.

CHAPTER THIRTY-SIX – HANNAH

"OH MY GOSH, THAT'S THE absolute perfect idea for Grampa's room!" I squeal.

"What is?" Palmer sneaks up beside me and puts her chin on my shoulder, peering at my laptop screen. "I let myself in."

I look at her sideways and smile. "You're just in time. I could use your style input. See this—putting his bed alongside the window so he can get light and his desk over here along the other wall so he can do his crosswords. Perfect." I point to the picture on Pinterest. "We'll totally have to put a bunch of photos on his desk, and maybe a corkboard over it, for him to put important things."

"Grampa uses a corkboard?" Palmer raises her eyebrows.

"Probably not," I say, secretly wondering why anyone wouldn't want a corkboard. "I promised Mom I'd arrange everything. She seems totally stressed." I snap my laptop shut.

"Completely and totally stressed," Sammie echoes, walking into the room. "She screamed at me this morning for not taking out the trash, only I had. And she growled at Owen when she tripped over a piece of Ziggy's dog food."

"Why Owen?"

"Because he'd filled Ziggy's bowl." Sammie widens her eyes.

"Sounds like you girls need to be on full 'avoid mom' mode. What can we do to help her out, so you two will be less under fire?" Palmer asks.

"Sam, you could set the table for her. She wants to use all the fancy stuff for Thanksgiving, but wouldn't get any of it out until the construction guys packed up last night," I suggest.

"I want to be with you guys." Sammie folds her arms over her chest.

"Here, Sam, I'll help you get the china down off the high shelves, get you started. When you're all done with the table, you can join us for the finishing touches, the fun stuff for your gramps." Palmer puts her hand on Sammie's shoulder.

"Deal." Sammie struts out of the room.

"Thank you," I mouth to Palmer.

She winks.

I work on clearing the remnants of the Tool Belt Crew from Grampa's new room: a scrap of carpet, some spare nails, and a tarp. Palmer reappears as I unwrap the crinkly plastic from the hospital bed.

"Sammie's so sweet. She wants to be just like you." Palmer grabs a corner of a flannel sheet with penguins on it Mom got at Target.

"More like she wants to be just like *you*. I know I want to be just like you. How did you convince her to leave us alone? You are so smooth!"

"Ha. Only with twelve-year-olds. I felt like such a loser saying good-bye to Kat. I told her, '*Adios, amiga*' and didn't even mention the whole how-in-the-world-are-you-going-to-handle-Thanksgiving-without-your-brother, and by the way, your mom's a jerk for not going to Spain with you."

I snort. Palmer always makes me laugh. "Right? It's like I have the right words in my mind, but I can't say any of them out loud to her. They all sound trite and awkward and like there's no way I could know what she's really feeling, because of course I can't."

Palmer shakes her head. "Turns out Claire's the bravest one of all. Who knew? It was really stand-up of her to share how she felt scared after the rape, and how she talked to a counselor. I don't think I could spill all of that. And I love her thankfulness thing." She tucks a corner of the sheet over the mattress. "These are really cute. I want some."

"I love the thankfulness list too. Only, I have to admit, I wish I'd thought of it. That is so up my alley, not Claire's." I pout. "Claire surprises me a lot. I thought she was ultra-cool when I met her. Then she showed up as fragile as Mom's china when school started, but she really has this inner strength, despite all the crap she's been through," I say, rubbing my hand on the soft fabric. "These'll be so snuggly and cheery for Grampa. The penguins can keep him company at night."

"He was pretty lonely, huh?"

"Really lonely." I flop on the bed, testing it for comfort. My eyes go to the wall, where we've scooted Grampa's new IKEA desk in the spot where our flat screen used to live. Something in my stomach tightens, a queasy feeling. "This has always been my favorite place to watch movies."

"We've had some great sleepovers here." Palmer sits next to me. "We totally memorized that cup thing from *Pitch Perfect* on the coffee table right here."

"Yeah, weird. No more sleepovers here. Unless we want to watch Ryan Gosling with Grampa."

"That might be fun." Palmer lies all the way down, letting her hair fan around her head.

I swat her.

"Joking. We get sleepovers every night at school now, in our own space."

"You're right. Like always." I sigh. "It's just cozy in here."

"It is cozy in here." Sammie crashes next to us and puts her head on my lap. "What will it be like with Grampa in our house all the time? I mean, I love him and all, but I'm used to cruising through here, and now it's going to be his room," Sammie says. "And what if I walk in on him when he's peeing?"

"Sammie!" I slap her playfully, although she makes a good point.

Palmer snorts and tugs Sammie's hair.

"Yikes, I just thought of that, like, just now," Sammie squeals.

We all laugh, and with Sammie's head on my stomach and Palmer's hair on my arm, we all seem to shake together, which makes me laugh harder.

"Sammie! Hannah!" Mom's voice booms from the garage as she stomps into the house. "Are you two done in here? I could *really* use some help getting the food ready for tomorrow."

"You can count on us, Mom. We've got you covered," I call, poking Sammie, clueing her to do the same.

She squints at me. "Uh, right, Mom. No prob."

"Me too, Mrs. Trager," Palmer adds. "I love to cook. Put me to work."

"That would be nice," Mom says, finding us on the bed. "Sorry I snapped, girls. I just want everything to be perfect for Grampa and Thanksgiving." Her sigh takes over the room. "This is going to be quite an adjustment. I want him to be happy." I see Mom force a smile to hide her tears.

I walk over and put my arms around her. "He'll be happy, Mom. Happy as a clam named Sam. He'll have us."

"Hey, I'm not a clam," Sammie says.

"Thanks, Hannah. You too, Palmer, and clam girl."

"Mom!" Sammie wails.

"Sorry. Sam the clam." Mom half laughs and walks toward the stairs. "Oh, and everything for the egg casserole is on the bottom shelf of the fridge. Make sure you use both bags of cheese."

"Got it," I try to reassure her.

"Hannah?" Mom's voice echoes from the staircase.

"Yeah?"

"Grab the trash can from your room for in here, will you? You're never here anyway."

My jaw twinges. I don't want to be selfish, but I love my PB Teen trash can. Grampa surely won't like purple? And I'm not ever here? I'm here now, but here keeps changing.

"Purple will clash in here." Palmer scowls.

I love that girl.

CHAPTER THIRTY-SEVEN – KAT

STRANGE MOUNTAINS RESEMBLING DRIZZLE SAND castles blow me away with their height and formation from the window of my train.

I detrain with locals making day trips, a school group, and a posse of pushy pilgrims making their journey to see the famous black Madonna supposedly carved by Luke, as in the gospel writer Luke. Everything about this place is straight out of a book. I wouldn't be surprised to see Robin Hood jump out of a tree, bow and arrow at the ready.

I inhale the cooler, fresher mountain air, appreciating a break from the city. There is an inexplicable energy vibrating through the streets of Barcelona, but I prefer air and space and room to run. I reposition the lump of my money belt and double-check my pocket for my phone.

Montserrat consists mainly of the abbey. But there are a few shops and cafés, plus my area of interest—the trails. I pick a two-mile trail that winds up and around to the cross of San Miguel. The muscles in my legs engage as I plod along the gravel path. I pass a scattering of fellow hikers, but mostly the path is all mine. There's so much space here. I breathe it in and hold it in my lungs before letting it escape again. I release my soccer ball from my bag. The trail is wide, and I dribble along for several minutes, pausing to juggle the ball on my knees and thighs, chest and insteps, exhilarated by each thud against my body.

A few strides forward and the path slants and narrows. "Time for you to go back inside," I tell my ball, kissing the leather and tucking it safely back in my bag.

My glutes and hamstrings appreciate the pull as I hike farther up and arrive at a crossroads. Uncertain of which way to go, I take a few steps in each direction, scouting what lies ahead, but still can't decide.

A murmur of voices comes from the left. I wait for them to catch up to me and smile at the approaching family.

"*Le cru?*" I ask.

"*Si. Por alli*," they answer liltingly, pointing from where they've just come.

"*Gracias*," I say, smiling and nodding my appreciation.

Just a few minutes down the left path and I see it. Set on the edge of what must be the highest mountain is a black metal cross, standing maybe ten feet high. A rail surrounds it, to keep people from falling thousands of feet over the perilous edge. I walk toward the cross in reverence, breathing in sunshine and earth.

The sun seems to shine directly on this spot. I let my skin absorb the warmth and light. I stand in silence, awed by the view of Barcelona resting in the valley below and by the arc of sand castle turrets four thousand feet above sea level. I lose all sense of time and space as I take in the expansiveness of it all—amazed that God created something so large, so tall, so beautiful.

I sink onto the concrete ledge at the base of the cross. And then I let myself do it. I actually let myself think of Alex.

I visualize the last time I saw him, other than at the hospital, when he dropped me off at school. I summon up the way his forehead creases when he grins and the sound of his hearty laugh. I bring to mind a spicy, musky cloud of Axe in the bathroom when it's finally my turn to get ready. I recall his rough hands passing me the carton of orange juice. I nod, remembering countless times he took an earbud and placed it in my ear so we could share a song. I shake with laughter and with sorrow and with joy and with love.

I hug my knees to my chest and remember how Alex held my hand when my parakeet died. I think of him singing in the shower, pulling the curtain back, poking out his head, and making funny faces at me while I brushed my teeth. I feel the force of all the times he pushed me into the swimming pool, and the sound of his laughter when I resurfaced.

I've been underwater for so long. Will I ever resurface?

My tears fall and my shoulders shake until I am as calm as the mountain I sit on. Empty. Drained. Warm from the sun, I wipe a stray tear that's settled in the crease by my nose ring. I close my eyes to rest.

The sun penetrates my eyelids, fracturing light and shooting prisms through my brain. Out of the pure blackness with streaks of indigo and lime behind my eyes comes Alex. He's far off, but there's no mistaking him. He wears jeans and a sweatshirt, and his head tilts ever so slightly. He walks toward me with his confident, but not cocky, stride. And with each step, the black and brights fade farther into the background and Alex comes clearer into view. He's only ten feet away now, and I see his smile. I smile too. I've been waiting for this. I knew he would come back to me. He had to.

CHAPTER THIRTY-EIGHT – CLAIRE

I FOLLOW THE WELCOMING SMELL of coffee down the winding staircase.

Walking into the kitchen is like walking into an episode of HGTV. Silver trays laden with scones and fresh fruit are on the right side of the granite counter. Two carafes with gorgeous white mugs, inviting me to wrap my fingers around them, sit on the left. The middle is arrayed with overlapping cloth napkins in gold, burgundy, and sage.

So, yes, moving here for the summer would totally work. I'd be living like a rock star.

"Nice of you to join us, Claire," Aunt Denise says in a disapproving voice.

Well, maybe.

"Good morning," Mom says.

"G'morning." I ruffle my curls, which seem to have exploded into Afro mode while I slept. They do that sometimes. Walking over to the table, I hug Mom. Her body is as small as mine, but it never has been a source of strength as much as something to cling to, a place to call home.

"My, you do have a lot of hair, don't you?" Aunt Denise interrupts my thoughts.

I nod, meander back to the food, and pour myself a mug of steaming java from the carafe marked with a little place card that says "Morning Blend" as opposed to the one next to it marked "Decaffeinated." Not even decaf, but the whole word. Auntie's jabs are the fine print on the shiny full-page ad promoting a new summer home. The only question is: Is it worth the jabs for the first-class service? Plus, she might not even want to take me in. That's a whole other issue.

"It's extra crazy in the mornings." I smile at Aunt Denise, tucking my mane behind my ears in an attempt to stay on her good side.

"Well, I'm sure you can tame it a bit once you've showered. Help yourself to breakfast, although we could almost call it lunch." Aunt Denise glances toward the clock, which reads 11:18 a.m.

Last I checked it *is* a holiday.

"Mission accomplished. The leaf is in the dining room table and the extra chairs are moved around it. What's next?" Uncle Chris rubs his meaty hands together, like he can't wait for another order from my aunt.

"If you could make sure you have out everything you need for your carving station." Aunt Denise raises one eyebrow higher than another. "I can't think of anything else we'll need until closer to dinnertime. I was planning on serving at four, since we had such a large breakfast, and it's good to let turkey sit. Oh, how about a fire?"

"I'm on it." Uncle Chris taps my back as he walks by. I shiver involuntarily.

"Looks like you could use a fire, Claire. You got the chills?" he asks.

"Sounds nice." I sip my coffee, hoping to find warmth in my cup. *Don't freak out*, I tell myself. "*You can't freak out every time someone touches you. He's your uncle, for crying out loud.*

I pour another splash of milk in my cup and add a sugar cube, always on a quest to replicate the *café au lait* I drank in Paris, then strategically sit between Mom and her sister, just in case Uncle Chris returns. "So where's Megan?" I ask, stirring my coffee.

"Who knows?" Aunt Denise waves her hand and laughs. "I can never keep track of her. She's so popular, you know."

Mom laughs nervously.

As if on cue, Megan slams the door.

"Hey." She nods to us. She's wearing the same outfit she wore last night, except her eyeliner is smudgier, her sweater is pulled down a bit lower revealing some serious cleavage, which I don't remember her having last year when we came to visit, and she smells like a walking cloud of incense.

"Happy Thanksgiving," Aunt Denise trills. "Have you had a chance to eat, sweetheart?"

"I'm good." Megan starts to head upstairs, then turns to the spread. "Well, now that you mention it." She piles her plate as if she's at an all-you-can-eat buffet, pours herself a mug of black coffee, and plops down across from me. Megan rests her feet on the table revealing the red undersides of her shoes, announcing they're Christian Louboutin's, which I only know from Palmer pointing them out to me in magazines. And I also know from Palmer they run about $800 a pair!

"I hate that incense." Aunt Denise waves her hand around as if clearing smoke from a fire.

"Mom, please," Megan says with her mouth full.

Mom shoots me a pained expression.

I shrug.

"So, Claire," Aunt Denise starts.

I count in my head the dried cherries nestled in my scone: one, two, three . . .

Aunt Denise doesn't get the hint. She clears her throat. "Dear, this is what I tell you every time I see you, look directly into someone's eyes when they speak to you."

"Sorry." I look up. Her eyes are this eerie bright blue, making them look like they were painted on her face. I can't hold her gaze long. I glance at my lap looking for my napkin, grab it, and wipe the corners of my mouth as a diversion.

"That's better." She licks her lips. "As I was saying, your mom was just telling me about your new apartment. It sounds," she pauses for effect, with Aunt Denise everything is for effect, "efficient."

"Where'd you move?" Meg shoves half a scone in her mouth.

"Oh." Mom's eyes widen. "I just moved closer to my school. I'm still unpacking boxes, figuring out where everything should go."

"That shouldn't take you too long, dear." Aunt Denise pats Mom's hand. "You said it's a one-bedroom, didn't you?"

Mom wrinkles her forehead. "Yes."

"If it only has one bedroom, where do you sleep?" Megan's eyes penetrate me.

"I haven't been there yet," I confess, pulling my hoodie tighter around me. "I've been at school, well, until yesterday, and then"—I half smile—"I came here."

"So where *will* you sleep?" Megan scowls. "That's kind of weird, don't you think? Not having a room? Not even seeing where you live?"

I look to Mom, half wanting to scream, "I told you so," half wanting to defend her. She looks flimsy. I tuck my hair behind my ears again, resolving not to push her over the edge.

"It made sense for Mom. I'm hardly around anyway." I echo her words from fall break. "I'm looking into options for the summer." My cheeks flush. I should have discussed this with Mom first.

"What kind of options?" The words rush from Aunt Denise's lips.

"I don't know yet." I take a bite of pineapple, the sweet juiciness spurting through my mouth. "Maybe getting a job and staying on campus, maybe staying with one of my roommates. Nothing for sure."

"I had no idea," Mom sputters.

"Me either, Mom." Her eyes are easier to look into than Aunt Denise's. "I'm not saying for sure. I wanted to talk to you about it this weekend, so I guess I am. I'm just saying, maybe. Maybe it would make sense."

Mom nods.

"Why don't you stay here?" Megan slurps her coffee. The whole room shrinks.

"I'd feel better if it was with family." Mom nods in agreement this time, not resignation.

"So, done?" Megan yawns. "I'm gonna take a nap."

"Okay, dear. We're feasting at four." The way Aunt Denise trills reminds me a little of Hannah, all perky and planny. I better warn Hannah to be careful. She does *not* want to turn into this.

"That would be such an opportunity for you, dear." Aunt Denise pats my hand. She's always patting Mom and me like we're poodles or something. It's kind of odd. "A chance in a lifetime." She spreads her arms out, motioning to her personal palace. "We'd have to work out ground rules, of course, but I'm sure we could make it work. After all, what are families for, if we can't help each other when we're down and out?"

"We're not exactly down and out," Mom says, "just crowded."

"Tomato, tomahto."

And just like that I have an official invite to spend this summer in the family Ritz. Perfect.

Right?

CHAPTER THIRTY-NINE – KAT

"KAT." HIS VOICE IS AS familiar as my own. Goose bumps sprout from my elbows and work their way up to my shoulders.

"Alex?" I know it's him, but I have to ask. He's so real, but . . .

"It's me. I promise." He leans down and hugs me, and he's warm like the sun. I feel the pressure of his body against mine. He's not a ghost. I can feel him.

He slides next to me, his head also leaning against the base of the cross. "I can't stay real long, but there are some things I need to tell you."

"You can't stay? You have to stay. Always." The word "always" comes out as a garbled whisper.

I grab his muscular arm. My fingers shake as they wrap around him, trying to grasp his solidness.

"Hey, I'm always with you. We're too tight for you to think for a second I'm not with you." Alex puts his hand under my chin and raises it, so I look him in the eyes. "You believe that, right?"

I nod, wanting to hold on to this second. I try to memorize everything about him.

"Are you . . . okay?" I ask.

"Look at me!" He grins. "I know you are worried. I know Mama and Daddy are worried, but I'm fine. You need to let them know I'm all right."

"Were you hurt?" I blurt. I've imagined him crushed and cut so many times, writhing in agony. I search his face for a scratch, a scar, some reminder of the accident, but there aren't any. It's just Alex. Just his face. Just him.

"Nope. Not a bit. It was all like lightning. The second I got hit it was over, well, actually it was all beginning. I got carried away. Lifted right out of there. Kat, that's what I need to tell you."

I'd imagined him terrified as the other car careened toward him, wondering how much it would hurt to have metal slice through my skin, to have a two-ton vehicle crash into my ribcage. But he's okay? Just like my dream where the dark stranger lifted him. Did Alex just say "carried"?

Alex's eyes twinkle like peridots, like they always do when he lets me in on a secret. "I have something really important to tell you."

Birds sing so brightly they sound like one of the bird callers on Las Ramblas. The sky is as blue as the stripes on FC Barcelona's jerseys. Everything is so vivid. I try to tune out the bombarding colors and sounds and focus on Alex.

"Right before the accident, that afternoon, I read this Bible verse from Ephesians 2, 'Saving is all his idea, and all his work. All we do is trust him enough to let him do it. It's God's gift from start to finish.'"

Alex's excitement is contagious. I feel tingly, like I've had too many shots of espresso.

He shrugs. "And then it all made sense. The trusting. The saving. He saved me. I mean, why would God make us if He didn't want to be with us? Why would He make these mountains"—Alex points behind him—"and this sky if He didn't want us to enjoy it? It's like, I'll always love you, Kat, even if you hog the hot water or eat the last cinnamon roll." Alex winks. "I'm not ever going to stop loving you and God's not either."

The anger that's been brewing inside me, that I've been keeping at bay, erupts now. I'm furious. "How can God love you? He *didn't* save you! He let you die. If there's a God, then He stole you from me!" The thoughts I've wrestled with since the night of the crash, the ones I've tried to bury with the pain, bubble from my lips.

"You can't look at it like that, Kat." Alex's lip twitches and his eyes well. "You can't. It's just for a while, sis. Wait till you meet Him."

"You've seen Him?" I ask. Shivering, I rub my hands up and down my arms.

Alex puts his arm around my shoulder. "That's what I needed to tell you. I'm all right. I'm better than all right. I'm in heaven." Alex's thick, full-bodied laughter fills the hilltop. "And by the way, the chai up there is way better than anything you've ever dreamed of tasting."

Chills creep down my spine. I untie my sweatshirt from my waist and pull it back over my head. Everything seems to be in slow motion as I'm immersed in the tunnel of fleece. How can he be here? I pop my head out, but he's gone.

I jerk my head and see Alex walking down the trail. He turns back. "You'll be all right, Kat. I love you, but don't forget what I said. Just keep leaning on that cross." He waves, turns, and keeps walking, a thread of string dangling from his pocket. Where he's going, I know I can't follow. I don't know how I know. I just know. But I do follow the thin line of string with my eyes all the way to my hand, where I grasp the other end.

CHAPTER FORTY – PALMER

AS I LIGHT THE SPICE tapers on the dining room table, Tia sets a bowl mounded with mashed potatoes in the center. A pat of butter melts, sending golden rivulets streaming down the sides. "I just love the smell of candles burning." She raises her eyebrows, then sticks her finger in the mashed potato bowl and licks the white fluff. "I love mashed potatoes too."

"Tia." I shoot her a disciplinary stare, but I don't really mean it.

She walks out of the room, and I slide the potatoes to one side, making room for the stuffing, turn the dimmer switch down, and set the linen napkins rolled in brass turkey napkin rings at each place. Perfect.

Jack Johnson serenades from the tiny speakers installed in the kitchen ceiling while I pull the sweet potatoes out of the oven, bubbly and tempting with marshmallows melting along the top.

Dad carries in the silver platter laden with turkey. "And now, what you've all been waiting for," he proclaims.

Mom surveys the table, checking off items in her head, literally nodding to each dish and serving spoon on the table. "Cranberries." She nods again. "Tia dear, grab the cranberries."

Mom, Dad, and I slip into our chairs. Everything smells golden and crispy and warm and slightly sweet. When Tia returns, Dad says, "Let's pray."

We hold hands, the four of us making a circle. Last year Keegan and I ate a brunch at his house before we had Thanksgiving dinner here. It was strange. They had turkey hash and omelets with salsa and sweet potato pancakes. I don't miss that brunch, or his parents. They always made me feel like I wasn't smart enough, talking about philosophers and politicians. But I do miss Keegan—his warm hand, at least.

Our circle had been five last year, and I remember thinking the circle would only grow when Keegan and I had kids. I scrunch my nose to get rid of the twinge.

"Thank You, Lord, for our family. For two beautiful girls, and the wealth and the health You've showered on us. Help us take these gifts and share them with others. Thank You for bringing Palmer home for this family celebration. Amen."

Dad nods and we let go of our hands. "I'll start," he says, referring to our tradition of listing things we're thankful for, kind of like our roomie list, but more public. "I'm thankful for a successful year with the business. We need to discuss as a family what charity we'll make a contribution to so we can share our wealth."

"Oh my gosh, I have the perfect one," Tia starts. "There's this orphanage in Rwanda—"

"Tia." Mom gives her the look, similar to the look I gave her when she tasted the taters. "Why don't we give suggestions after everyone has said what they are thankful for. You go next."

"Yeah. Right. Sorry." Tia looks down, but I can tell she's stifling a laugh, which makes me have to suck in my lips. "Okay, so I'm thankful Palm is home." She tilts her head at me.

"Thanks."

"And I'm thankful my tennis team made it to States, and for Thunder, 'cause she's a cutie, and for Black Friday, 'cause I cannot wait to go shopping tomorrow." Her eyes light up. "And I can't wait to talk about this orphanage in Rwanda, because it's really neat what this guy is doing there, you know, to help people who were affected by the genocide."

"All right. All right." Dad chuckles. "Honey?"

"I'm thankful we're all together. I'm thankful for my book club and my gardening club. I don't know what I'd do without those ladies. I'm also thankful for Raoul's successful year, and all his hard work to provide for this family." Mom smiles at Dad, and although they are usually two separate entities to me—Mom and Dad—in this moment, in the candlelight, I can see how much she loves him. And when Dad looks at her, his dark eyes filled with emotion, I see the love coming right back at her, something deeper than what Keegan and I ever had, something richer.

My eyes well out of gratitude for my parents happiness, especially after seeing what's going on with Kat's family, and jealousy of what they have and what I've lost, and hopefulness that God has someone else in store for me.

"Palmer." Mom squeezes my hand.

I swallow and sit up a bit straighter. "I'm thankful Mom and Dad are in love." I smile at them. Dad's mouth opens slightly and Mom's eyebrows rise. I'm sure I've never told them that before. "I'm thankful for time with Tia." I want to say I'm thankful for our pinkie pact, but that's private, just between us, but just thinking about it sends a warm sensation across my heart. "And I'm thankful for my roommates and for God's plans, whatever they are."

I do have plans for you, Palmer. Don't worry.

Not Keegan? I ask God, although the answer is already crystal clear.

It never was.

"Amen," Dad announces; translation: dig in.

"Amen," we echo back.

We pass plates clockwise. I select the cranberries I simmered with orange peel and cloves last night for my first bite. They are sweet and tangy and spicy on my tongue. And that same inviting steam that enveloped me from the cranberry pot last night envelops me again, but this time I know what I'm feeling is God's love.

And I am thankful.

Thankful for this room. This family. This food.

And for now, that really is enough.

CHAPTER FORTY-ONE – KAT

I HEAR VOICES. IS ALEX coming back?

I squint in the direction of the sound, but don't see anyone. Everything is dark and blurry like when I get my pupils dilated at the eye doctor's office. The voices get louder, but I can't decipher the Spanish. I lean forward, remembering Daddy's words of caution. The whole teenage girl alone in a foreign country bit. I focus on widening my eyes harder and harder, until—*pop*, they open!

My eyes were closed. I'm curled up on the ground by the foot of the cross. Did I sleep? I still smell Axe mingled with chlorine. I rub the bumpy concrete with my right hand where Alex was sitting, as if it's a genie's lamp that can make him reappear. How can I still smell him? He seemed so real, more vivid than anything I've ever experienced.

He was too real to be a dream, but too incredible to be real.

I sit up, my eyes darting to where Alex disappeared. No glimpse of him, just four Spaniards meandering up the path—the voices that snapped me back to reality.

Checking to make sure my money belt is secure and my phone is in my pouch, I stand. One last whiff of Axe and chlorine brushes my nose. These guys *look* nice enough. They're probably about my age, but four guys against one girl makes this not the best place for me to be.

Time to move on, my inner voice tells me.

Maybe it's not only time to leave this spot, but also to leave the bitter sadness that's engulfed me for weeks, constantly rearing its head just when I thought I'd pulled myself together. Maybe it's time to let go of the anger toward God. To let myself heal.

My mind pulls back to Alex. What was he telling me? Why did he come now? After all of these days of me missing him?

He never felt the pain, even though he looked a mess in the hospital. I sigh. Like a weight lifter dropping her barbell, I feel so much lighter. I've carried around the weight of his fear and pain, but they never existed.

You can let go.

My inner voice is loud.

But can I?

My feet swish along the gravel lining the trail. The group is almost upon me, but they're not even looking at me. They're consumed by their own conversation, and I'm immersed in the conversation I've just had with Alex.

I shake my head. It all sounds like a book or a hokey movie or a . . . I nod to myself . . . a dream. That was it, just some crazy, weird dream from the sun and the elevation going to my head.

The guys are directly in front of me. They stop, and I twitch. *Remain calm*, I tell myself. I smile to show a sign of friendliness to feign confidence.

The shortest one of them with sleek black hair and bangs cut straight across his forehead wears a gold cross around his neck. It glints in the sunlight. He smiles, and they walk on.

A cross.

I walk with deliberate steps. Their voices fade as the space between us widens. I relax, still shaking away my fog.

Fumbling to find my ringing phone, I flick it out of my pocket and check the ID. It's Daddy.

"Hey," I blurt.

"Hey, sugar. Remember our text on the hour agreement? I'm on a break from my meetings and wanted to see how you were getting along. Everything all right?"

"Oh, sorry, Daddy. I was hiking, and I think I dozed off. And, uh, sure. I'm fine."

"You fell asleep hiking? That's hard to do. You sure you're okay? You sound funny, maybe it's these international airwaves."

"I'm fine, Daddy. I came up to Montserrat. The signal's probably not so great on this trail."

"How is it? You bein' smart?"

"It's beautiful, Daddy. Spectacular. And yes." I glance over my shoulder, where the group of guys take pictures of each other around the cross. "I'm bein' safe." I speed up my pace, as if doing so will get me to the important part of my story faster. "It's amazin'. I have so much to tell you. I hiked up to this cross, and I saw Alex. I mean, I had a dream, sort of, and he was in it, and he wanted us to know he's okay."

Silence. I take the phone from my ear and check to make sure I still have a signal. Everything looks all right.

"Daddy, you there?"

"Eh, emm," Daddy clears his throat. "You're alone? Are you really all right? Where are you now, sugar?"

"I'm almost back to the monastery, just walkin' down the path. Oh, Daddy, it must sound crazy," I say. "I felt pulled up to this cross, and now I know why. It was because Alex wanted to talk to me there."

"You said you dreamed all that?"

"It wasn't really a dream. I mean, there's a whole lot more. I'll tell you about it, but Alex really wanted you and Mama to know he's all right. He didn't want you to worry anymore."

"Mm-hm." Daddy sounds far away. I can't tell if he's thinking about Alex or about how crazy I am.

"You did this dreamin' by yourself, on the top of that mountain?"

"Yeah, I closed my eyes in the sun and nodded off. It's so peaceful here, but it wasn't like a dream I made up; it was like real, like a way for Alex to talk to me." The more I talk, the more insane I sound. Why would anyone believe me? By the cross, it was so clear, so obvious. It seems with each step I take I get further and further away from the truth.

"You eat anything strange this mornin'?"

I flash to the churros and chocolate. "N-no," I sputter.

"Probably the sun got to you or the height or somethin'. Glad you're all right now. I'll meet you at four, just like we planned." Daddy tries to talk himself and me out of believing in my conversation with Alex. "Why don't we meet at McDonald's? Some American food might clear your head."

Daddy hasn't suggested McDonald's since when we were little, and we'd get sweet teas on Saturday mornings on our way to my soccer games or Alex's swim meets. He's definitely worried.

"McD's? Really?"

"Might as well. It's easy to find. You remember where it is?"

"Got it."

"All right, then. I need to be gettin' back to work. See you at four." Daddy sounds flustered.

"Yes, sir. I promise."

Click.

I stare at my phone.

It's like Daddy let all the words about Alex just float past his head. I know I sound crazy, but I touched Alex. I smelled him. He told me I'd be all right too, if I keep leaning on the cross. It's been so hard to focus on God, with all He let happen. But Alex said it wasn't like that. It wasn't God hurting Alex, but bringing Alex to be with Him.

I finally have some of the answers I've been seeking, but they raise so many more questions. I feel like a rock climber who, after some serious reaches and stretches, has made it up to a great foothold, only to take a breath of air so I can keep climbing onward toward the goal—the top.

I allow myself the thought of his name, the flash of his face, the brightness of his smile. Alex is okay. I let the beautiful reality sink in, after weeks of thickening my armor layer by layer to avoid the pain. It's hard to truly accept happiness. But after seeing, smelling, hearing, and touching him again, my fears and anxieties start to peel away like a snake shedding its skin.

"Lean on the cross," Alex said.

I'll try.

CHAPTER FORTY-TWO – HANNAH

"WACE YOU!" MY THREE-YEAR-old cousin, Hadley, and his twin, Harley, thunder past me—a flurry of sticky fingers and sneakers, shaking the floor so hard I almost drop the green Jell-O I'm clearing from the table.

Woof woof! Ziggy chases after them, always up for a race.

"Chill," my older cousin, Tate, says, then returns to the intense phone call he's having with I'm assuming one of his harem of girlfriends. He is strangely attractive, in a Daniel Radcliffe, schoolboy sort of way, but he's my cousin, so technically that's gross. Plus, he's a womanizer, so even grosser. Apparently his innocent persona, that's not actually so innocent from the stories Mom tells me, has a magnetic pull. Regardless, I couldn't help flirting with him over Thanksgiving dinner. I told myself I was just using it as practice for a real boy. But the way his hazel eyes glinted at me behind his glasses was kind of sexy. Enough. I shake my head at my irrational thought process.

Sammie and two of our tween cousins pull crumbles out of the almost empty pan of stuffing, chewing and giggling and glancing at Tate, thinking he doesn't notice.

I pick a maraschino cherry from the Jell-O before sliding the bowl in the fridge.

Mom swooshes past me, her face tense.

"Everything was delicious, Mom." I beam. "I mean, over-the-top amazing. The turkey was juicy, and I loved the way you sprinkled toasted pecans on the sweet potatoes. Yum. Everyone was talking about them."

"Thanks." Mom looks tired. "The pecans were a good addition, weren't they?"

"As tasty as can be." I smile, tossing leftover dinner rolls into a giant Ziploc baggie. "But the rolls are always my favorite." I tap the smooth plastic. "Well, and the pies."

"Pies will be in a little bit. When I get the rest of this cleared away. Could you put a pot of coffee on for me?" Mom exhales loudly.

"Sure." I put the bag of rolls in the bread drawer and turn to the cupboard. "I think Grampa is having a good time."

Mom nods. "I think so." But she doesn't look like she thinks so.

"He ate a lot, took seconds on things, and he laughed a lot."

"I know." Mom's forehead wrinkles. "I'm just nervous about not taking him back to the nursing home. The part where he stays here."

"When are you going to tell him?" I ask, pouring fragrant hazelnut coffee into the filter.

"When are you going to tell who what?" Grampa asks, rolling himself into the kitchen. "Oh, good. Coffee. I was just coming to see if I could drum some up. Perfect with pumpkin pie, you know. Well, with whipped cream and pumpkin pie."

"Maybe we can put whipped cream in our coffee?" I suggest.

"Maybe." Mom sighs.

"Definitely." Grampa grins. "It's Thanksgiving, after all. Now, what were you two conspiring about?"

I look to Mom, who looks about five years older than when I went away to school two months ago. The wrinkles around her mouth are deeper set. Dark shadows encircle her eyes.

She needs a Palmer makeover. And a trip to a spa. And to worry less.

"Well, Dad." She puts down her glass on the counter with a surprising clang. "We have something we want to tell you."

"Everything okay? Hannah, you didn't fail out of school? Owen's not sick or anything?"

Grampa looks older too. Dark spots pepper the skin on his hands, and his hairline looks like it's receded another inch, maybe two. Has everyone been taking aging serum while I've been away? Did they look like this before and I didn't notice? Does being away emphasize their age? Or has Grampa's fall been the beginning of a downward spiral for everyone?

Maybe to soothe Grampa, or maybe to reassure myself, I rub his arm. His sweater is fluffy, but under the knit his arm feels bony. "Nothing like that, Grampa. I just got an A on my Botany exam, and I got a B+ with the chance to do revisions on my English paper."

"Well done, Hannah." He rolls himself back an inch, then forward again.

Dad walks in carrying the gravy boat. "Best gravy ever, dear."

Mom looks down.

"You say that every year." I laugh, answering for her.

"I mean it every year." Dad ruffles my hair, which makes me cringe, because I spent at least forty-five minutes trying to straighten it this morning. Dad is clueless in the hair department. I try to inconspicuously smooth it back with my hands.

Mom looks at Dad, then me, then toward the dining room full of relatives, then back to Grampa.

"Your dad was asking what was going on." Mom's eyes implore Dad. "Hannah and I were going to tell him."

"I wish someone would tell me." Grampa's energy from a minute ago seems zapped, as though he anticipates something ominous.

"We don't like you staying in the nursing home, Dad." Mom's voice softens.

"Well, that makes two of us," Grampa grunts. "Bunch of old people groaning and moaning. It's depressing."

I laugh out loud. "Exactly, Grampa."

He winks at me, his blue eyes resuming some of their spark.

"So . . ." Dad drags out his syllable like a sports announcer. "We've set up a room for you here. We want you to stay with us." His words come out in slow motion. He hooks Mom's arm and walks toward the old playroom/Grampa's new bedroom before the *s* in the word *us* falls off his lips.

I follow.

But Grampa doesn't.

"Grampa?" I turn to see if he needs help wheeling himself.

His face is blank. He shows no sign of moving forward or backward. He is frozen.

"Grampa?" I ask again, putting myself in front of his gaze.

"Oh, yes, yes." He nods and sets his hands on his wheels.

A cold tingle runs down my arms. Grampa isn't happy. He should be so happy. This is all for him. Maybe he doesn't understand.

Once in the room I talk to fill the awkward silence stretching to every inch of the newly carpeted floors. "So, this is your bed. Aren't the penguins the cutest? And this is your crossword desk. You can use it for anything, but I thought we could do the puzzle tomorrow, I mean, I'm still here, and you'll be here." I tap the stack of paperback crossword books.

Mom and Dad examine Grampa's face. Grampa stares at the desk. Everyone looks like they're waiting for something.

So I keep going. "I thought about putting a corkboard up for you, to pin stuff on, but Palmer didn't think you'd really use one. So, if you want one, let me know, and if not, we'll leave it like this. And I put pictures up." I smile. "One of me, of course."

But Grampa's face doesn't register emotion. And he still hasn't said a word.

"And of Sammie and Owen too. And the other grandkids. We got them from your house. The ones you had by your bed there. I figured they must be your favorites."

Grampa buries his hands in his face and lets out a low moan, like he's been hit in the stomach. What did I say? I was trying to show him how great this is. I look to Mom, but she pats her hair and sucks in her lips. I look at Dad, but he furrows his brow and rocks back on his heels.

All of my turkey and gravy and potatoes are doing somersaults in my stomach, and all my words are doing flips in my brain. The only time I ever saw Grampa cry was at Gramma's funeral.

Why doesn't Mom or Dad make him stop? Why don't they chime in about all the work they did to make this so perfect? Mom's planning? The money Dad paid? It still smells like fresh paint. I even gave up my trash can, after all, so he'd feel at home here.

"It's for the best," Dad says, his voice echoing off the walls.

"You don't want to go back to the nursing home, do you, Grampa?" I plead. "I thought you said it was depressing." I feel my eyebrows hugging my skull.

"I just want to go home." He shudders.

CHAPTER FORTY-THREE – CLAIRE

I HAVE THE SENSATION OF being in a crowded, packed-so-tight-I-can't-move elevator with someone's shoulder in my face. Everyone's wearing perfume or eau de body odor and then the elevator lurches.

My stomach is uncomfortably stuffed. Aunt Denise's caterer must have spent hours concocting the sauces alone. And I'm restless to get away from the table. My aunt and uncle present long, detailed rants on the upcoming school levy and how it will affect their property taxes. The only interruptions of their drone are Aunt Denise's etiquette tips for me. "Don't play with your hair at the table, dear," and "Claire, a young lady should express her political views. What do you think of the recent levy?" The only view I have right now is how I can't wait for the virtual elevator doors to open so I can charge out onto the next floor.

I toss my hair from one shoulder to the other. Oops.

"Thank you for dinner." I place my napkin neatly on the table next to my plate. "It was incredible. Where would you like me to put my dishes? Do they go in the dishwasher?"

"Heavens, no. The gold leaf would chip." Aunt Denise shudders. "Let the help clear them, dear. That's why they're here tonight, so we can all sit back and give thanks without having to worry about chores."

In the kitchen three workers bustle. I hear the distinctive *pop* of a champagne cork.

"Are you sure?"

"Absolutely. Sit tight. Sounds like the champagne will be poured momentarily." Aunt Denise's eyebrows waggle.

"And hopefully the scotch," Uncle Chris pipes in.

"Of course, dear. Whatever anyone would like."

The last time I tricked myself into thinking I could handle a glass or two of wine, I couldn't. "I'm so full I don't think I even have room for a sip of water," I say. "I might go for a walk, if that's okay." I bat my eyelashes at my aunt, knowing she loves to be sucked up to. "I want to make some room for those delicious desserts I saw. You do everything first class, Aunt Denise."

Her chest swells in pride. "Thank you, dear."

"I'll join you on a walk, Claire." Mom stands.

THE OUTSIDE AIR HITS ME like a snowball, cold and damp and instant on my forehead first, then my cheeks, then everywhere. I wrap my scarf around my neck, button my denim jacket, and slip thick gloves over my fingers. I shudder at the chill, but revel in the escape.

"It seems like winter's arrived." Mom stuffs her hands in her pockets as we walk into the wind.

"It still feels good out here." I nod. "It was really stuffy in there. Maybe I ate too much."

"Denise can take up a lot of room," Mom says flatly.

I let out a soft laugh.

"I didn't mean to be unkind," Mom apologizes.

"I know." I snort. "I just envisioned her puffing up like Violet Beauregarde in *Willy Wonka*, literally taking up a lot of room. I know what you mean, though."

"So, you sure you want to live with them this summer?" Mom asks, keeping her eyes trained on the sidewalk.

"I'm not sure of anything."

I taste a thick, smoldering smokiness on my tongue. "Someone's having a fire."

"Smells like it." Mom's boots shuffle through scattered leaves on the sidewalk. "Chris will have one roaring by the time we get back." She puts her arm in mine. "You know, sweetie, if you lived here this summer, you'd have your own room with a fancy king-sized bed, Egyptian cotton towels, and gourmet food. Goodness' sake, even the hand soap in the bathroom is imported."

"I know, right? Did you smell that stuff? Infused with lavender from Provence. I wanted to jump into the bottle and swim around for a while."

Mom laughs. "I'm sure you could get a job around here. But I'd miss you. Summer's my downtime. I know I usually teach a couple workshops, but I was looking forward to having you home. Maybe I could come up here for a few days . . ."

"Just because Megan thinks it's a done deal doesn't mean it is." I twist a ponytail holder through my curls, pulling the weight of my hair off my shoulders. "I didn't mean for it to come out in front of Megan and Aunt Denise. I'd been thinking about options for this summer, and then when I got here, it was hard not to consider how nice it might be to stay here. But I also thought about staying at school and working there or maybe crashing with Hannah or Palmer."

Mom takes a short breath.

"And I hadn't ruled out staying with you, Mom." I tilt my head on her shoulder, which is hard to do while walking, but somehow feels right. "I don't know. Everything's changed. It's different being away at school. I know we didn't see each other tons between your schedule and mine, but we were both still there, you know? I knew you were around. And now I haven't even seen your new place, but I am happy for you." I lift my head to make it easier to walk. "I really am."

I mean it this time. I didn't before, but I see in Mom's desperate eyes she really needs this new place. "But just because your apartment is perfect for you, doesn't mean it will be perfect for me. Does that make sense?"

Mom nods.

My thoughts weave from Palmer's fancy house to Aunt Denise's chateau, burdened by the social price tags and expectations of both. Could I be myself in either of their homes? Could I come and go as I please and find time alone? My mind wafts back to Mom's and my place, where we used to live, and fades into my impression of Mom's new apartment. Like the smoke streaming from the chimney of Aunt Denise's house as we circle the block, my heart orbits the rooms of each option, trying to find a couch I can curl up on, a place I can call home.

CHAPTER FORTY-FOUR – KAT

ABOUT FIVE ZILLION FOLKS ARE crammed into McDonald's at 3:55 p.m. To avoid the mobs of people and trash cans and trays, I wait for Daddy out front, rehearsing how I'll relay to him my afternoon with Alex.

Daddy hustles toward me. "Sorry, sugar. The crowds to get on the metro were so thick we didn't all fit on the first train. I had to wait for the second one." He lurches into me as someone pushes past us, clamoring toward the smell of deep fryers. "Doesn't look much less crowded in here."

I pat my thighs with my palms. "It's insane. Should we go somewhere else?"

"Sure." Daddy shakes his head. "Just thought it'd be an easy place to meet."

I snort. "Who knew Mickey D's would have such a cult following in Spain?"

We pick our way through the crowd, searching for a spot to eat. "I think it's busy everywhere in Barcelona. I remember it was before, but I didn't remember it being this congested. How about here?" Daddy points to clusters of silver and red chairs and tables spilling out of a restaurant called Qu Qu.

"Looks fun." I shrug. "At least it's fun to say."

We order a sampling of Spanish tapas from the menu: risotto, prosciutto, something with mushrooms (we recognized the word *funghi*, but that was it), and a dish of olives and cheeses. When the waiter leaves, I inhale, nervous, but ready to tell Daddy everything. Before I can start he chimes in.

"So, tomorrow is my day with my little girl. What do you want to see? The Picasso Museum? Parc Güell? The beaches where they held the Olympics a few years back?" Daddy pulls a stack of colorful brochures from his briefcase. "There's Sagrada Familia and the Chocolate Museum."

"Did you say Chocolate Museum?"

"Mm-hm. Here it is." Daddy holds up a pamphlet with pictures of sculptures made completely out of chocolate.

"Wow." I twirl my pinkie ring. "Do you get to eat any?"

"You must." Daddy opens the cover.

"Daddy."

"Yeah," he murmurs, immersed in tourist literature.

"All right. Here goes." I drum a beat with my thumbs on the café table. "On the mountain today Alex told me to lean on the cross, and then when I was walking down from the cross, some guy was wearing a gold cross. Don't you think that's wild?" Okay, not at all what I rehearsed, but it's a start.

"Lots of people wear crosses, sugar." Daddy reaches across the table and feels my forehead. "I really think the elevation up there got to you."

"Daddy, it was not the elevation." I swallow hard, angry with myself for such a lame explanation. Why can't my words match what happened? "I saw Alex!"

"Kat, it's good to have strong memories of Alex. But our minds play funny tricks on us sometimes. You've traveled far. There's a significant time change. You might just be tired." Daddy pats my hand.

"Dang it. Why won't you believe me?" I ask, knowing why. Knowing I sound ludicrous. Warm tears pool in the corners of my eyes. I pull my hand away.

Our waiter arrives, halting my attempt to explain what I saw. What did I see? I stare at the ground, searching for answers, while he scatters small plates on our table.

By the time he walks away, I'm more confused than when I started.

"Let's pretend we're restaurant reviewers." Daddy does a one-eighty with the conversation topic, bringing up a game we used to play when Alex and I were little. "I'll start," he says, not giving me a chance to explain myself, or maybe giving me the chance to regroup. He takes small bites from each of the plates. I copy him, trying to sort my thoughts while I taste.

I exhale.

Daddy clears his throat.

"The risotto with a smooth, cheesy sauce is my favorite, my ten out of ten." His voice is deep and rich, like a John Grisham lawyer.

"The cold pickled mushroom thing only earns a one. Rubbery with a hint of puke taste," I announce in a voice like James Bond's.

"I wouldn't have rated it that highly." Daddy blinks, scrunching his mouth.

Bubbles from my carbonated water spurt up my nose. I wipe my face and lean back. Daddy looks at me funny. I'm not sure if it's because I'm snorting

Pellegrino, because of the chewy mushroom, or because he thinks I'm going nutso.

"I really did see him, Daddy."

"I know you wanted to."

I shrink. "Was it eerie? Yes. Crazy-weird? Definitely! But it was real. It had to be."

"Goodness knows I want to believe you." Daddy rubs his chin. "I have to admit, I've been looking for him ever since I talked to you, half expecting Alex to jump on the subway or pass me on the street."

I spin my pinkie ring round and round. The words I struggled with before now roll off my tongue. "I didn't see Alex because I wanted to. I mean, I've wanted to since the day he died, but I saw him today because *he* wanted me to. He had something to tell me. He wanted me to tell you, Daddy. He wanted you to know he's okay."

"He's okay." Daddy shakes his head. "He's okay." Then he turns solid, like stone, and his voice morphs into a harsh whisper. "He's dead, Kat. My boy is dead, and there is nothing okay with that."

My stomach tightens. But then I hear God in my head. It must be God, because I wouldn't have thought it on my own. *Tell him why Alex is all right.*

I look up from the table, back at Daddy. "He's okay, Daddy. Alex said he's okay, because he's with Jesus."

Daddy looks at me like I've streaked across the field naked at halftime of an Alabama game.

"Alex didn't feel any pain. He wasn't hurt. He said Jesus just whisked him away, and now he's having a blast in heaven."

Daddy stabs a ball of mozzarella with his fork.

"And, Daddy, I had this other dream, before, back at home, before we even came here, of this man carrying Alex's body out of the crash and upward. And Nicholas told me how chai lattes are like heaven and now it all makes sense, don't you see?"

Daddy shakes his head. "Dreams? Lattes? Kat? Listen to yourself, girl."

I want Daddy to believe me, but would I believe me? Do I make sense? Probably not. It's taken me a long time to get to this place. Maybe Daddy needs more time.

I look at him. His face is twisted. His fingers are wound around each other. His heart must be wounded like mine was. I want to help him.

God, please?

CHAPTER FORTY-FIVE – PALMER

THE BALL HITS THE SWEET spot in my racquet as I lob it over the net.

It sails over my head and bounces in the farthest outside corner of the court.

"Game point," Hannah calls, bouncing a yellow ball, once, twice, then swinging her racquet, sending the ball squarely in front of me. I return it with my backhand. She swooshes it back up and to the right. I reach as high as my arm will extend and smash it over the net. She races to the ball, but not in time.

"Game," I gasp.

"You totally whooped me!" Hannah puts her arm around my shoulder as we walk off the indoor courts at the club.

"Ha. Barely." I laugh, wrapping my arm around her waist. "Tia's playing Varsity this year, and she's gotten way better than me. Can't stand it."

"Can't stand she's gotten good, or can't stand that your little sister is better than you?" Hannah swings her racquet as we head toward the café.

"Yeah, well." I click my tongue. "Something like that."

"No matter which Ruscilli sister is better on the tennis court, I'm glad you're the one who is my roommate."

"Thanks, Han." I kiss her cheek, then turn to the worker.

"What can I get you?"

Of all the people on the planet to be working the café at the club the day after Thanksgiving, it's Carly. She's wearing a sports bra and ultra-short athletic shorts. For real? It's November. She could catch pneumonia! It's hard to look anywhere except the cleavage staring me in the face.

"Vitamin Water Zero," I say coldly, turning my eyes to the Styrofoam cup with the word "TIPS" scrawled in pen. *Gag.* "Do you have Rise?"

"Dunno. Is that the pink kind?" She picks up a file and starts sawing her nails. Puh-lease. I'm all for a perfect mani, but while you're taking someone's order? Not to mention they're clearly acrylic and painted a tacky yellow caution-tape color with blue and green rhinestones glued to the tips.

"No, it's orange, like orange juice." Goose bumps prickle my sweat.

"Take whatever kind you want." Her eyes are still on her nails.

Zzz-zzt, zzz-zzt, the sound of the file pricks the back of my neck.

"You want me to serve myself." I try to control my voice.

"I'm kinda busy." She looks up from under her bright blue eyeliner. "Oh, it's you."

"I got it." Hannah slips in front of me, grabs two plastic bottles from the fridge, and hands one to me.

"We'll just put it on the Ruscillis' account. Do you need me to sign?" Hannah steps up to Carly. "Or are you *too busy*?"

Carly tilts her head, keeping her eyes on me. This close I notice she has acne with an inch of foundation plastered over it. Not particularly pretty, and she apparently took a bath in cheap perfume, because the overpowering sweetness churns my stomach.

"Maybe you're too busy screwing my boyfriend." The words fly from my lips before I know what I'm saying. Hannah clutches my arm and tries to steer me away.

"You don't know what you're missing, priss." Carly licks her lips. Like in a really gross, Lady Gaga kind of uncomfortable way. "Keegan is dee-licious, if you know what I mean."

"Come on." Hannah tugs.

I resist for a minute, gawking at the Kardashian-like quality of Carly. I'm tempted to spit at her. Instead, I spurt, "Only a tramp would know what you mean," then turn away.

I'm shaking, like a bottle rocket with a lit fuse on the verge of launching.

"You have got to get out of here," Hannah says through her teeth.

"I can't believe I just said that." I cover my mouth, my chill overtaken by a searing heat. "It's not her fault Keegan's a dirt bag." I gasp for air, shivering, sweating, and sobbing as soon as I'm certain I'm out of Carly's view.

"What am I gonna do?" I sink into the couch of the ladies' lounge where Hannah's dragged me. She hands me my North Face from my bag and helps me slide into it.

"I don't want to get back together with him. Especially now—not after . . ." I can't even say her name. ". . . her."

"Remember we decided he's not the guy for you anyway?" Hannah opens my water, the plastic seal cracking, and hands it to me.

I swallow the cool sweetness, letting it settle my insides as it slides down my throat. "Mm-hm." I nod, but my legs bounce up and down uncontrollably. "So why is he with *her*?"

Hannah blows her hair out of her eyes. "I'll give you two guesses."

I snort through the tears. Snot comes out of my nose. "Ew." I laugh more and jump to the sink to grab a tissue.

I look in the mirror. "Double ew! Look at me! No wonder he wants Carly."

Hannah's by my side. "Be serious, Palm. Did you see her? There's only one thing he wants from Carly, and it's only because he's ticked he can't have the real deal. That's you."

"Really?"

"You know it." Hannah's reflection nods at mine. "You're beautiful and smart. He's desperate and angry, and apparently indiscriminate."

"I know." I blow my nose again. "But it still sucks. Not to mention I'm a total jerk for talking to her like that. Why can't I ever control the things that pop out of my mouth?"

"Let's shower, pick up our little sisters, and hit the mall for some Black Friday action. You can tell me more about the editor guy from *QuadAngles*." Hannah unzips her gym bag. "Did you say his name is Matthew?

"Michael." I dab the mascara smears out from under my eyes. "His name is Michael."

CHAPTER FORTY-SIX – HANNNAH

I FLIP BACK TWO PAGES in my notebook and consult my to-do list. I'm always thankful for placing a check next to something, like *finishing my English paper* last night—totally boring, but totally done. And *completing my Theories of Learning assignment* this morning, before I even went down for breakfast. I smile with a sense of satisfaction as I jot down my accomplishments on my thankful page.

I try to focus on the positive, but my mind rewinds to Grampa's tears Thanksgiving night. He's downstairs somewhere. I barely saw him yesterday, between tennis and shopping. When I got home from the mall and dinner, Mom and Dad were in his room with the door closed, speaking in hushed voices. Grampa never came out afterward, and they wouldn't talk about it. I hate to admit it, but I'm using my homework and thankful list as stall tactics to avoid having to face whatever's going on down there.

While I make a dot on my paper for my next thankful item, Ziggy barrels into my room, huffing and puffing. She scoots next to me and sticks her face on my lap. Her fur is cold. "Have you been outside already this morning, girl?" I ask, rubbing under her silky ears. "That's right. You like that, don't you?"

She whines, thumping her tail against my arm.

"Breakfast time? I thought so too. Give me just a minute."

After brushing my teeth, yanking my wavy hair into a pony, and pulling on a sweatshirt, I call, "Come on, girl. Let's go see what we can find."

Bounding down the stairs, Ziggy and I halt in the kitchen. Grampa sits alone in his wheelchair in the middle of the room. He looks frail. Where is everybody? Why is he unattended? Does he need help? Is he okay? What if I can't help him? *God, a little help here.*

"Hannah?" Grampa registers me staring at him. The sun shines through the kitchen window and glints off his sparkly eyes.

"It's me. You okay?" I ask, stepping forward and giving him a quick hug. I'm too chicken to mention his talk with Mom and Dad, or to ask if he was okay sleeping here the last two nights in a strange bed, or if he still wishes he were home.

"What? Yes." He nods, hugging lightly back. "I'm fine."

"Good." I use the most chipper voice I can muster. "Have you eaten breakfast yet? I know it's, like, impossible to fathom, after everything I've eaten over break, but I woke up completely starved. Crazy, right? I'm pretty sure there's leftover coffee cake somewhere around here. Let's see where Mom stashed it." I fill the empty kitchen with words, opening cupboards and pulling down plates and glasses. I pour two glasses of juice, and I ramble some more. "Where is everybody? Have you seen Sammie or Owen?"

"I think Owen's playing one of those crazy video games. Not a word from Sammie. Your mom and dad have zipped past a few times. Something about yard work." He shakes his head, like we're all lunatics.

Ziggy barks softly.

"I know. I didn't forget about you, Ziggy. Just a sec." I rummage through the pantry for the heavy bag of dog food, hoist it, and let the meaty chunks thud into Ziggy's bowl. Ziggy charges the bowl like she's never been fed before. "There." I slide my hand along Ziggy's soft back. "You're taken care of." I turn to the sink to wash my hands.

"You sure are on the move," Grampa says, wheeling himself toward the table.

"I try to be."

"What's all the hustle about? You don't go back to school today, do you?" His voice has a slight shake on every word, like his vocal chords are rattling around in there. I can't help stealing a glimpse at his throat. It looks normal enough.

"No. No. Not yet. I'm just hungry, is all. And I bet you are too. And Ziggy was. And I have a lot to get done today so I'll be ready to go back. Some more homework, laundry, packing. Oh, look, someone did make coffee. I thought I smelled it. Well, they didn't leave us much. How do you take yours?" I swirl the quarter-full pot and look at Grampa in his striped pajamas. I should know the answer.

"I'd really rather have tea," he says.

"Me too." I set down the pot and pause.

Warmth creeps from my heart, up to my sternum, and melts upward through my throat into a smile; not the clipped, pasted-on hurried smile from a second ago, but a real one. A real smile for the real way I love my real grampa.

"I think we have peppermint, chamomile, and cinnamon spice."

"You pick." Grampa's words come slowly, like they're in no hurry at all. Not being frazzled sounds nice. Just on Wednesday I told Palmer, Kat, and Claire how excited I was to be going home to get a break from classes and meetings and my ongoing search for the perfect boy—well, I never truly take a break from that. But ever since I've been home I've been doing. Baking and decorating and shopping and getting caught up on everything, everything but relaxing. Maybe Grampa's onto something.

"Cinnamon spice is my *favorite*." I pull down the box of tea and reach for the glass pitcher to heat up water in the microwave, but reconsider. Why not use the teapot on the stove? I have all day.

While the water boils, I find and heat up the coffee cake, placing it on little plates with cartoon turkeys painted on them. I peel a couple of clementines, laughing when the juice squirts me on the nose. I sneak a sweet, tangy section and hand one to Grampa, who's content looking out the window at a cardinal flitting from branch to branch. Maybe I'll get him a birdfeeder for Christmas so he can hang it outside this window and bird watch whenever he wants. That might make him feel more at home here.

The teapot whistles, shooting steam into the air. Despite the shrillness, I find it comforting, a signal of readiness. So am I. Ready to sit and sip warm tea with my grampa while we solve the weekend crossword.

CHAPTER FORTY-SEVEN – KAT

A RAINBOW SPANS THE COUNTER: explosive orange, vivid red strawberry, bright green kiwi, stark white coconut, sunny yellow pineapple, and even neon pink passion fruit juices, freshly squeezed in clear plastic cups. They look too luscious to pass.

I select a pineapple-coconut blend. Daddy goes with strawberry-banana. We slurp the thick sweetness through straws and swap sips while struggling to stay together through the throng of morning merchants and shoppers.

"I like mine better."

"Me too." Daddy smirks. "Tomorrow I'm gettin' that kind."

"Tomorrow we should both get different kinds, to try more." I nudge him. This is so non-Thanksgivingy, but somehow just right. There's a pang in my ribcage as I think of Mama with her sister and Alex gone—well, up in heaven. *Do you eat turkey in heaven?* I wonder, looking upward.

I don't get an answer, but the sky above is bright blue. The sun is warm on my face.

Thank You, God, for this day. For sweet, exotic juice on my tongue. I want to taste every kind of juice and see every site imaginable. Suddenly I feel I can fill up my thankful journal, the one that was so difficult to even write one line in the other morning. I'll miss Alex.

Always. But he'd want me to seize this day and the one after it and the one after that.

We buy pastries for now and baguettes for later, stuffing the long loaves of bread in my string bag so the tops peek out like babies from their packs.

We don't say it out loud, but it's understood Daddy and I will stay on the move all day to avoid longings for Mama's cornbread stuffing and for Alex's jokes. We visit the Chocolate Museum, where the ticket is a real chocolate bar, and we tour Camp Nou, Barcelona's famous soccer stadium.

"I can't believe we just saw the actual locker rooms Messi changes in, the turf where Valdes tends goal! Thank you, Daddy! It was amazin'," I tell him while we ride the metro.

"My pleasure, sugar. Maybe someday I'll come see you play there."

We both lurch as the train stops at the centerpiece of Barcelona, Sagrada Familia. The cathedral is so tall, they say it can be seen from anywhere in the city. Modeled after the sand castle drip structure of the mountains of Montserrat, the cathedral is unpredictable in a majestic way. Scaffolding and cranes litter the outside of the upmost turrets, cranking away toward the estimated final completion in 2026.

The basilica's construction began in 1882, but still isn't finished. Kind of like me working on dealing with losing Alex. I'm working on it, but definitely not finished.

"I've never seen a church like this before," I say as we inch through the line.

Walking inside is like walking into the land of the Sugarplum Fairy. The walls are spun sugar white and the stained glass isn't dark and serious, but more like the colors of lollipops. Looking up at the overlapping beams and designs reminds me of lying on the floor of a forest and gazing at interlaced tree branches. Gleaming wire sculptures encase backlit colored glass, tributes to the authors of the four gospels. The whole place glows with a modern, spiritual magic.

I find a vacant seat and let my mind drift. Curly, polished balconies and tour guides holding signs blur in my vision into undefined brightness and color and space.

Happy Thanksgiving, Kat. I hear God's voice in my heart.

I miss Alex, I answer.

I know. I can almost sense God nodding, as if He truly does know how I feel.

I'm okay, and then I'm not. A tear sizzles down my cheek. I swallow. Dang, I thought I was better.

You are. It's going to take time. Things are going to be different.

I dig in my pocket for a Kleenex and blow my nose. I breathe deeply. I don't want it to take time. But in a way, I guess I do want it to take time. I don't want to *not* miss Alex. I just want it to hurt less.

It will. In time. I'll be right here.

CHAPTER FORTY-EIGHT – CLAIRE

"WHA-AT?" MEGAN YAWNS, REMOVING HER headphones so she can hear me.

"I've gotta catch the bus back to school."

"Did you have to say the word *school*? I have an entire paper to write before Monday on why Monet painted differently from everyone else and why that was so important. Talk about painful."

I sit next to her on her bed. "Monet?"

"Yeah, that French guy, one of the Impressionists."

"I know. I saw his painting, well, his biggest one, *Les Nymphéas*, when I was in Paris." I bring back the beautiful swirls of every blue in the spectrum, pinks from pale to fuchsia, and seafoam greens to the forefront of my mind.

"Wanna write the paper for me? I'd let you borrow some of my clothes this summer." Her lips curl upward, like a fox trying to trick a chicken.

"No thanks." I shake my head, feeling my braids shift along my back. "I have to finish reading *East of Eden* and write a paper on it by Monday."

"That entire Steinbeck novel? How far in are you?"

"About half. I figure I can finish it on the bus ride home, but I'll still need to write the paper. Sometimes I think college is just a really expensive place to read."

Megan laughs. "I'm with you on that. You're funny, Claire. I still might let you borrow my clothes."

"Thanks." I adjust my bag on my shoulder. "The reason it was important Monet painted differently, if you want my opinion?" I check her expression.

"Go on."

"Well, everyone else was painting things exactly like they looked, which takes talent, to make something look absolutely real."

Megan nods.

"But Monet went a step further. He painted the way light looked on an object, how the light changed it. So he didn't paint water always blue or green, even though that's how we see it or think we see it or even how it really is."

"Huh?"

"Okay." I drop my bag to the floor. This could take a minute. "When light shines on a lake, it reflects and refracts. Then the water appears yellow or white in spots, maybe orange from the sun or even red. Monet focused on the light's effect on an object, not on the object itself. So he used choppy strokes and vibrant colors. All the Impressionists did, each in their own way. And because Monet, and the others, painted differently, everyone else thought they were wrong. But different doesn't have to be wrong. Sometimes different can be exciting. Sometimes it can be the start of something altogether revolutionary."

Megan stares at me, her eyes clearer than they've been all week. Her mouth looks tight, not arrogant, but thoughtful. "That's really beautiful, Claire. I forgot how smart you are. For being so under the radar, you're actually pretty cool." She gets up from her bed and grabs a peach-and-ivory filmy dress from her closet with the tags from Anthropologie still attached.

"Here. It's way too flower child for me anyway. So not my look."

"You sure?" I ask, letting my fingers slip across the delicate fabric.

"It's so much more you."

It is definitely me. I can already picture it with my cowboy boots and a long string of glass beads.

Megan slides her MacBook onto her lap and types while repeating my words, "Different doesn't have to be wrong. Sometimes it can be exciting. Sometimes it can be the start of something altogether revolutionary." She snaps it shut. "I think I have the first line of my paper."

I nod.

I think I have a new way of looking at Mom's move. Maybe, just maybe, it will be the start of something revolutionary.

CHAPTER FORTY-NINE – PALMER

I SIT ON MY SUITCASE, crammed with new clothes, trying to get it to zip. I bounce a little, not wanting it to break, and rock back and forth. There, almost.

Boom.

I slide off the back and onto the floor.

"Ouch!" I rub my behind, already sore from the walk Tia, Mom, and I went on this morning. I thought we were going out for a mother/daughter stroll, but Mom walks like it's an Olympic event. She mentioned more than once how good exercise is for a woman's figure, then glanced at me.

My phone buzzes. I fumble to standing and find it in the zippered pouch of my purse.

Going back today. Can I see you one more time?

Is he serious? "Uh. NO!" I scream, deleting Keegan's text and sliding my phone back in my purse.

I pounce with a fierceness on my suitcase, which pops into place, allowing me to zip it. "There." I snarl at whatever forces were keeping me from shutting it before. Well, the snarl is really for Keegan, but he's not here to hear it.

I spot my journal under my chair. It must have fallen. "I cannot forget you." I rush over, like it's the love of my life, and rub my hand along the cover. Sitting on my bed, I open to the page I've marked with a silver bookmark. Quickly I scrawl:

I AM THANKFUL FOR:
   - A suitcase that zips shut
   - New clothes that make it a challenge to zip, especially the black cashmere sweater, and the new pair of Lucky jeans, because they accentuate my curves despite Mom's comments, and the cool new scarf, well, all of them

I tap my nails on the page.

   - A fresh manicure
   - The ability to ignore Keegan's texts
   - Going back to school today

I pause and chew on my pen, careful my lips don't touch the edges so my caramel lip gloss won't smear. I underline the part about ignoring Keegan. Hmm . . . what do I have to look forward to back at school? I'm so ready to go back!

   - Roommates—all of them: Claire, Kat, Hannah
   - Cups of tea on the futon
   - Magazine staff meeting on Monday, which means new assignment and Michael
   - The potential of Michael

Another text buzzes. I close my journal and clutch it to my chest, ignoring my phone. But what if it's Hannah? I'm supposed to pick her up in a little bit to drive back to school. Or Kat with news from Barcelona? Or Claire letting us know she got on the bus okay?

I slip my journal in my purse, trading it for my phone.

Palm. I know you're mad about the Carly thing. She said you were pretty evil at the club. ☺ You're gorgeous when you're mad. I don't like her. I love you.

He loves me.

I sink back into my bed, afraid my rubbery legs won't hold. I flutter my lashes, warning the wetness in my eyes not to surface. Do I have time to see him, just for a second before I pick up Hannah? I mean, if we left ten or fifteen minutes later for Clarkston, it wouldn't make that big a difference, would it?

"Mom said you're leaving?" Tia's in my doorway. "I don't want you to go. Stay?" She plops down next to me and gives me puppy dog eyes.

"I'll be back in three weeks for Christmas. And then I'll stay for almost a month." I hug her, still clutching my phone.

"All right," she groans.

My phone vibrates again, reminding me of Keegan's text I didn't clear or respond to.

"Is that Hannah?" Tia tilts her head.

"Keegan."

"What did he say?"

I hold up my phone for her to see.

"What a jerk." Tia grabs the phone. "Can I text him back?"

"Tee," I warn.

"Palmer, God has better plans for you."

"It's not that easy. I know you're right. I know that's true when you and I talk about it." I look to the ceiling. "But part of me . . . I just feel all weak and jumbled."

Tia's almond-shaped eyes stare back at mine.

"Would you pray with me?" I beg. This isn't something we normally do, but something about it feels right.

"Yes. Yes. Yes." Tia grabs my hands. "But you have to pray for me too."

"Deal." I nod, comforted by the weight of her thin fingers in mine. "Dear God, please give me strength. I know now, finally, that Keegan is not 'the one.' He couldn't be. He's making it hard for me to be true to You." I exhale. "I used to laugh at all of that stuff about temptation, like that wasn't real, but it is. I feel so out of control when I see him or kiss him, so far away from You, God." There's a tremor in my throat. "Help me remember how he was falling over Carly at Starbucks, and that is so not what I want or need. And be with Carly too." I shrug. "Help her make good choices. And I am sorry I was so evil to her. Forgive me? Anyway, please help me get over him. Completely over him, God. Please help make it be easier."

I can't bat the tears away any longer, but these aren't the tears of longing and heartbreak I avoided a minute ago. These are tears of love.

Tia squeezes my hands, offering some of the strength I lack and reminding me of our bargain. "And be with Tia as she looks forward to the dance. Help her have a great time, but make good choices, remembering how awesome she is always, and that she never has to make compromises."

"You either," she sputters, wiping a tear. "Thanks, Palm. I don't know what I'd do without you."

"Amen." I look up at my sister, who is becoming more and more of a friend. "You help me all the time."

Zzzup.

"I'm gonna kill him!" Tia roars.

"Have at it." I hand her the phone.

"Oh my gosh, Palm," Tia squeals. "Look!"

She hands me my phone and I read:

Hey, it's Michael. Hope you had a good turkey day. Want to grab coffee before staff Monday night?

CHAPTER FIFTY – HANNAH

"OH MY GOSH, ARE THESE chocolate chip?" Palmer walks in my kitchen and points to the platter of cookies on the counter.

"Yeah. My aunt brought them for Thanksgiving, which is so weird, right, because we have pumpkin pie and apple pie every year, and don't get me wrong, chocolate chip cookies are awesome, although I think oatmeal raisin are my favorite, but she knows we have pie and she brought these anyway. They weren't on the menu."

"So, I can have one?" Palmer's plum nails dangle over the plate.

"Sure. Help yourself. Did you get your nails done? Pretty!"

She beams, spreading out her fingers and gazing at them. "Yup. A little therapy after the whole Carly disaster. Tia and I got our nails done yesterday. It's gel. Hopefully it'll last till Christmas break when I can get them done again."

"Well, hello, gorgeous." Grampa wheels his way into the kitchen.

"Hi, Mr. Trager." Palmer hugs him. "How exciting you're living here. Hannah told me all about it. How's your hip doing?"

She speaks to him as naturally as if she were talking to me or Kat or Claire. How does she do that? I have to think about what I say to him, plan it out, and he's *my* grampa.

"Oh, it's all right." He nods. "The pain comes and goes. What are you girls nibbling on?" He cranes to see what's on the counter.

"Chocolate chip cookies. And they're really good." Palmer sweeps up the plate and carries it over to him like a waitress, well, hostess.

"Thank you, dear. I forget your name."

Awkward.

I contract my ribs. Grampa's met Palmer before. I hope she doesn't think he's deaf or loony, just because he's in a wheelchair. Because I noticed over Thanksgiving, everyone yells things at him. Stupid things like, "The gravy's good, isn't it, Dad?" I mean, if Grampa liked the gravy, he could comment on it, and gravy is so not worth screaming to be heard about. I vowed not to talk to Grampa like that—all condescending—so I analyze everything I say so I don't say it too loudly or talk down to him, and I take so long thinking about it, I end up not saying the right things, the normal things, quickly enough.

"It's Palmer." Palmer winks. "We've met a few times. Like at graduation. But there were so many people there."

She doesn't miss a beat. Another thing to be jealous about Palmer.

"Well, I shouldn't forget a face as pretty as yours." Grampa selects a cookie from the side of the tray, one that's tucked under two others.

"You got a good one." Palmer winks again. "One with loads of chocolate chips. You're a man after my own heart."

"I'm going to take my cookie and go sit where there's some sunshine. Nice seeing you again, Palmer." Grampa turns his chair and puts his hands on the wheels.

"You too. Hopefully I'll see you again over Christmas."

"I'll look forward to it," Grampa says as he rolls himself out of the kitchen, pausing at the little bump in the threshold, but managing just fine.

"It must be fun having him here." Palmer picks chocolate chips out of the cookie she's holding one by one and pops them in her mouth. "He's so cute."

How does she avoid getting crumbs stuck to her lipstick?

"I love Grampa." I open the fridge decorated with alphabet magnets anchoring various Crayola drawn turkeys, Popsicle stick pilgrims, and a sketch of a horn of plenty. I pour two glasses of milk. "But things are different, ya know?"

"Well sure," Palmer says.

The milk glugs and fills the clear space, turning it white. "Like these glasses." I turn one in my hand. "When you pour milk in them, they totally change. They'll need washing and you can't even tell they were clear and sparkling and sitting neatly in the cupboard, and . . ." I shake my head.

Palmer scrunches her forehead while cutting another chip out of the base of the cookie with her fingernail. "What?"

"I have no idea what I'm saying." I collapse in the nearest chair and chug the creamy milk. "Everything's different. That's all. And I'm so bad at different."

Palmer brushes some of the crumbles she's made from her cookie dissection off the counter and into her hand, tossing them down the drain. "You like everything neat and tidy and this isn't. It's different and messy."

I nod. Sometimes it's scary how well she knows me. "It's not bad. I'm really happy he's here. He's my favorite person in my whole family, besides Mom, Dad, Sammie, and Owen, I mean, outside our immediate family. We've always had something special, but I don't know how to act around him. You were so good with him just now. So smooth, normal. I totally fail. Epically. It's like I forget how to talk." I exhale, feeling myself flush.

"You? Forget how to talk? Doubtful." Palmer waves her hands around.

I laugh, but it's a lame laugh. "Right. Totally weird. But you saw me just now. You chatted away while I stood here like a mute. I'm elated he's here. There's nowhere I'd rather have him be. But I don't know if I should talk about his wheelchair or not, and Grampa wants to go home, so I don't know how to tell him how happy I am he's here, because I don't want him to think about the fact he's here when he doesn't really want to be." I take another swallow of milk.

"You way overanalyze things, Han." Palmer eyes her cookie, finds one last morsel of chocolate, eats it, and tosses the remains in her napkin and her napkin in the trash.

"What did you just do to that cookie?"

"You saw?"

"Hard not to."

Palmer flips her wrist dramatically. "Mom has been less than subtle about the fact she thinks I've put on a few pounds. This is my way of getting all the best part of a cookie, without all of the calories. I figure I left out most of the buttery, eggy, sugary part." She pats her stomach.

"You do not have to worry about your weight. Can you stop with that, already?"

"See, you can totally talk straight to me." Palmer sits back with perfect posture and crosses her legs. "So, tell it straight to Gramps. He's sharp and funny. Just be you. Tell him you love him. He'll appreciate that."

I stand and rinse my glass, the water turning the glass clear again, back to its original self.

Just be me. Sounds easy enough.

CHAPTER FIFTY-ONE – KAT

THE KITCHEN LOOKS THE SAME. Same smooth shiny wooden floors. Same four cane-back chairs at the round table by the window. Same counters with same bowl of fruit sitting on the end. I don't know what I expected.

I am so different. The world seems so different. I guess I expected everything to be different, but the house looks the same.

"Baby, we're home!" Daddy calls.

Silence is his only answer.

I scan the room, waiting for Mama to emerge from the opening by the hallway or to pop out of the bathroom, but she doesn't. The entire house feels dark and empty.

"Guess she's not here," Daddy says in a hollow voice.

"You told her when we'd be back, right?"

"I told her." Daddy tenses his jaw as he sets our luggage on the floor and rubs his temples.

"What the—" I stop myself for Daddy's sake, but I can't stop the tears. I can't believe we traveled half way across the world, didn't spend Thanksgiving together, and she's not here. Didn't she miss us? Isn't she glad we're back? How could she do this to me and to poor

Daddy? I look at him, so full of life yesterday, like a soccer ball that needs an air pump today. At least Daddy is real. He talks and he cries and he smiles and he frowns. I can't remember the last time Mama did anything.

"I'm sorry." I hug Daddy.

"It's all right." Daddy rubs my back. "She's got to do things in her own way."

I think about that. Daddy and I both felt pulled to go to Barcelona. I know why I had to go. It's where Alex wanted to talk to me. I can't tell if it helped Daddy or not, but I think in some small way it did. It sure beat moping around here on Thanksgiving. Maybe Mama didn't need this trip like I did, or maybe she needs something else. Anyway, I hope she finds it real soon.

"I'm going to call her," Daddy mumbles, walking toward his office.

"I'm headed upstairs."

It's strange, but I feel the need to tell Daddy where I'm going in our own house. I guess it was so important on our trip to let each other know where we were. It got to be a habit.

I hesitate outside Alex's door. The TV hasn't been turned on in a long time. The clothes haven't been worn. I let go of the handle of my roller bag. My eye catches on his bookshelf; along with dozens of other titles sits his Bible.

I walk toward it like a golfer approaching the tee, excited, nervous, cautious, full of concentration. I slide the leather volume from its slot. Dust flurries light and gray.

A bookmark is creased between the paper-thin pages. My fingers tremble as they open to the marked page, Psalm 34.

I read.

If things aren't going well, hear this and be happy:

I swallow. Hard.

Sinking into his bed, I keep reading, absorbing every word. It's eerie. Like a message for me, but I didn't see it until now.

God met me more than halfway,
he freed me from my anxious fears . . .

Is this legit? It's like these pages speak directly to me. I can't read the words fast enough. I skip down a few lines.

Is anyone crying for help? God is listening,
Ready to rescue you.
If your heart is broken, you'll find God right there

My heart is broken. *But, God, You're right here. I know it.* The anger I felt toward Mama, the tenseness, fades. My muscles tight from travel loosen.

My face is wet and warm and drenched.

"Alex," I sputter, "did you leave this for me?" The room is silent. The house is silent, but I know the answer. It can't be an accident. Seeing Alex and now this—I don't believe it's a coincidence. There is purpose in finding this book marked to this page.

My finger traces up the words to the beginning of the passage, words Alex highlighted in yellow, "*I live and breathe God; if things aren't going well, hear this and be happy.*"

I am warm all the way through. I am overwhelmed with emotion like I might erupt. Tears gush from my eyes and my body shakes, but I am no longer desolate, thinking about the vacancy in Alex's room, or the absence of Mama, but instead, overwhelmed by all the love that lives here.

CHAPTER FIFTY-TWO – KAT

"THE PICS YOU POSTED REMIND me of Paris." Claire folds her legs crisscross style.

"They were amazing." Hannah nods. "But let's talk about those in a sec. Claire, you want to go first? The thankfulness list was your idea, after all? Oh, I almost forgot, M&M's for all my friends." Hannah pours a mega bag of the candies, all red and green ones, into a bowl with reindeer dancing around the rim.

"Not me." Claire slips her hand in and out of the bowl, scooping up a handful of candies stealth-like, almost unnoticed.

"Weren't we painting pumpkins here just a few days ago?" I ask. "Where do you get all this stuff, Han?"

"Hannah has a way with the holidays. She's like a little fairy." Palmer winks at Hannah, who curtsies and blushes just enough to turn the edges of her freckles pink.

Silence falls over the group. Everyone's waiting.

"I'll go first." Palmer pulls out her journal, opens it exaggeratedly to a marked page, runs her finger down the lines, turns the page, exhales, and shuts it softly, setting it on her lap. She looks down at the journal like she's forgotten what she's doing, but I'm pretty sure it's all for effect. She suddenly sits up and squares her shoulders like she's going to give a presentation. "I'm thankful it's totally over between me and Keegan. For good this time." Palmer pops one red M&M on her tongue.

Hannah eyes her.

"Truly. I'm good with this." Palmer nods. "Mostly." She raises one eyebrow. "So none of you can ever let me call or text him. Ever. Not even in my weakest moments."

"How about Skype?" Claire asks, twisting a strand of hair.

"Ha!" Palmer throws an M&M at her, and it falls down her flowered blouse. "No Skype either."

"Oh!" Claire's mouth makes the same shape as the sound it made, and we all laugh while she rummages around in her shirt and pulls out the candy. "Wasn't much to stop it down there." She laughs, holding the M&M in the air like a trophy.

"And I'm thankful my mom's moving."

"Bu—" Hannah tries to interrupt, but stops when Claire continues.

"It gives me the chance for something remarkable to happen. I've lived in the same place forever. But what if something new means something better?"

"Cheers to that." Palmer holds an M&M up in the air and clicks it against one of Claire's in a toast.

Claire's lips curl. "One possibility is my aunt invited me to stay in her mansion this summer, which would be luxurious, but comes with some serious family tension. Or . . ." She twirls another loose curl around her pinkie finger. "I might stay here at Clarkston if I can get a job with the university for the summer, or, I don't know, maybe something else awaits me."

"What are you going to do about Christmas?" Hannah asks. "Because you could totally come home with me. That would be the best Christmas gift, Claire Bear, but my grampa's there, so you'd have to stay in my room with me, but we're used to rooming together, right? We could shop and bake and craft. We always make this awesome advent wreath. Oh, crud." Hannah buries her face in her freckly hands. "I guess they'll make it before we get there. Advent starts next weekend!" She looks up, her eyes widening. "We could make our own Advent wreath here. Please, please, please!"

"Your Christmas sounds fun." Claire's eyes dance. "But I promised Mom I'd spend Christmas with her at her new apartment. We're going to decorate it together. We can still make the wreath, though." She takes one red and one green M&M from her hand and eats them. "I still might stay with Mom this summer. That's not out of the realm of possibilities. I'm just open." She crunches the chocolates. "And praying."

"We'll pray too." Hannah nods. "You have such a great attitude. I freak without concrete plans. And I'm awful at change. I totally struggled with Grampa moving in, which is way easier than your mom moving."

"Not easier." Palmer rubs Hannah's back. "Just different."

I drop a few M&M's on my tongue. I let them sit there until they slowly dissolve, melting chocolate throughout my mouth, reminding me of my *chocolata a la tassa* from just days ago, although it seems like weeks, or maybe years.

"Right." Hannah exhales loudly. "Well, thanks to Palmer, I'm able to say I'm thankful Grampa is in a wheelchair." Hannah looks at Palmer and gives her a secret look. They do that a lot. Not intentionally, not to exclude Claire and me. They just go way back, and sometimes it makes me feel out of place. Not tonight, though. Tonight feels good—being back here, surrounded by their glances and chatter and expressions and Claire's hair and soft laughter and all of the vibrancy of it, like our dorm room is alive, our friendship actually has a heart that beats.

"I don't get it?" Claire's voice is soft.

"Me either." I shake my head.

"I don't mean it like *that*. I mean, I'm really sorry he broke his hip, but because Grampa broke his hip means he gets to live with us; better yet, that I get to live with him. I was really freaking out about him not being able to do all the stuff he used to do, and not knowing how to act around him, and I'm still not totally sure." She tucks her feet under her. "But before I left, I told Grampa how much I love him, and how excited I am I'll get to wake up every day of Christmas break in the same house as him. He got a little misty-eyed, which is so sweet." Hannah clutches her chest. "And Grampa said he was glad too. That it sure beat waking up by himself every morning wondering if it was Tuesday or Wednesday because there wasn't anyone to ask." Hannah imitates her grampa's voice.

"Not that he forgot what day it was. I just think he was lonely. So even though he misses his house, which makes me sad, he doesn't miss being alone. He'll have us, and we'll have him, and that makes me feel warm inside." Now Hannah's eyes are all dewy as she rubs her heart.

"Come on, Kat. Stories. You haven't said a peep, and you're the one who went to *Spain*. We're dying over here." Palmer throws her hands in the air. "Oh. Dang it.

Sorry. I didn't mean to say that." Palmer looks like there's an M&M or ten or twenty stuck in her throat.

"It's all right." I shake my head, knowing she would never intentionally say "die." It's just what people say. I'll get used to it. "Well . . ."

I've been sitting here, laughing, listening, watching my roommates like I'm viewing a YouTube video, but now I have to engage, and I'm not sure how. I've read Psalm 34 over and over. It gives me a strange kind of peace. But still, I wish Alex were here to tell my story with me. It should be us sharing the stories of our crazy Thanksgiving trip to Barcelona. But instead, it's just me. I bite my tongue, look to the floor and back to my friends.

"Well," I try again. Claire takes my hand in hers, and I don't pull away. Palmer is on the other side of me and takes my other hand. Our fingers interlace, and my indigo polish makes an alternating pattern with her plum fingertips. It's comforting to be touched, not stifling like it felt before. Hannah's intense expression softens. The words from the psalm echo in my head, *God met me more than halfway, he freed me from my anxious fears.*

"How about the food?" Palmer squeezes my hand. "You sent that picture of hot cocoa. I've been craving some ever since."

I swallow. "Right. Funny. I was just thinking about that. *Chocolata a la tassa.* Chocolate of the cup. It's the first thing I wrote on my thankful list. It tastes more like a glass of hot fudge than cocoa, and when you dip these little pastries called churros in it . . . mmm." I nod. I'm finding my groove. It feels good to share these things. The things I tasted and smelled and heard and felt. "Barcelona is crazy and buzzy and busy, all the time. We jammed in as much as we could in the few days we had.

Daddy and I went to the Chocolate Museum and the mecca of all soccer, the FC Barcelona stadium, which was awesome. We went to the most beautiful church ever, Sagrada Familia. We even saw some pickpockets."

"Really?" Claire shivers. "At the church?"

"Really. And no. On the metro. They tried to steal some old lady's purse, but she stopped them."

"Good for her!" Hannah shouts. "Did they get arrested? How'd she stop them? What did you do? Weren't you so scared?"

"I don't know, she just held on tight, I guess. And it was weird for a second, but then it was kind of funny and almost cool, 'cause she'd single-handedly stopped a whole gang of pickpockets." I take a deep breath, gearing up for the most important part. "But something way crazier happened. Like, so crazy, you'll never believe it."

There it is. The start. I need to lay the whole story out for my friends to see. I let go of their hands, because my palms are damp with sweat. I twirl my thumb ring. Daddy still coddles me when I try to bring it up, and when Mama finally appeared, I tried to tell her, but she just looked right through me like I was made of steam.

"What happened," Hannah asks, scooching in closer, tightening our circle.

"All right, I know it sounds crazy, but I hiked up this mountain, and while I was on the top, I kind of fell asleep against this giant cross. The cross overlooks miles and miles of mountains." I grab my phone and flip through pictures, finding one of the cross at Montserrat and pass it around.

"Wow," Palmer says.

"Okay, there was nothing like that in Paris." Claire passes the phone to Hannah.

"I am so jealous. Don't tell me. Some beautiful Spanish boy named Pablo or something kissed you and woke you up, like Sleeping Beauty." Hannah makes kissy lips.

"Better." I laugh. "I saw Alex."

My friends give me their full attention, away from the M&M's and the picture on my phone and their hair and their nails, right at me, but not with a "Kat's lost her mind" look, like I had feared. Instead, they look at me like they're waiting to hear what I'll say next. Like this is as real a part of my story as the churros or the soccer stadium.

"So it was sort of like a dream, only it wasn't, 'cause Alex answered all these questions I had, and I could smell the chlorine that always clings to him after he swims, and the things he said I couldn't have dreamed up if I tried." The words tumble.

"What'd he say?" Claire asks.

"He said he was all right. He said I shouldn't worry." My words are thicker now, getting jammed in my throat, but I want to push them out. I have to keep talking, even though each syllable propels tears from my eyes. "He said he didn't feel any pain." I pause to inhale—a long sweet, deep breath, because this is the clincher. "He said he's in heaven."

"That's beautiful." Claire rubs my knee.

"You saw him? And talked to him? And smelled him?" Hannah whispers.

I nod.

My friends exchange glances, words without sounds.

"We knew he was in heaven. Right?" Palmer scoots even closer.

"Yeah. But heaven seemed so vague, so out there, ya know?" Emotion pricks my nose. "Was heaven the sky or a state of mind or how long did it take to get there? I sure didn't know. I couldn't picture Alex up there. I could only picture him here." I swat a tear that landed on the tiny stud in my nose. "But now it's real. Vivid. I don't assume he's there. I *know* he is."

"Wow." Hannah's shortest sentence ever. She stares into my eyes like she's trying to pull something out of them.

"I'm all goose bumpy, Kat." Palmer has tiny tears in the corners of her eyes too.

"Me too." Claire hugs herself tight.

I lean against the futon in awe of my friends. They don't question my kooky story. They believe me. They trust me that much. That's exactly what I needed to feel at peace today.

Embrace peace. Don't let it get away! God keeps an eye on His friends.

There's that psalm, resounding in my ears again.

"Here's to Alex." Hannah raises an M&M.

The tiny clacks of candy shells warm the room.

"To Alex," Claire echoes.

"And to friends," I choke. "Best friends."

It's Addicting
By Laura L. Smith

CHAPTER ONE—PALMER

"DO WE DARE WRITE A feature on Shamrock Saturday for our next issue?" Summer, the features editor for the school magazine *QuadAngles*, finishes tapping something onto her tablet and looks up.

I stand near some stools by the kitchen counter in Summer's apartment, praying I don't look as awkward as I feel. Awkward is not my thing. I am the girl who always knows exactly where to sit. I am the girl everyone wants to sit next to…at least I was. The university magazine staff doesn't care about my past popularity, or my $2,000 orthodontist-perfected teeth, waxed eyebrows, and fresh manicure. It's not the sort of club you just sign up for. I've been on staff since last year, but have never had even one of my stories end up in the actual magazine. After a trial article I submitted was nixed, I was relegated to the dreary office on the third floor of the English building to work on edits, layouts, and selling ads. But somehow I landed an invite to attend the first editorial meeting of the semester tonight at Summer's. Does it mean they want me to write? Have I paid my dues? Was everyone invited? Or was my e-mail address accidentally on the list?

Uncertain, I called home for advice. Dad answered, which is usually a good thing. But not this time.

"If they don't want you one hundred percent, you don't want them," he bellowed. "I remember my first sales job. They wanted me to work only on commission, no investment in me. I told them to get lost. Within a week I'd found a job with full salary and benefits. Gotta go where we're wanted. All in. Maybe writing isn't your thing. You should go into sales like me. Lots of money in sales. You have the perfect personality for it, and heck, how could anyone *not* buy something from you?"

"Maybe," I'd said as tears he couldn't see slid down my face.

If they don't want me? I don't do "not being wanted." That's for someone else. And so is sales. I hated selling ads for the high school yearbook and pumpkin pies for the tennis team fund-raisers. I felt like a nerd calling my own aunts and uncles. I could never ask strangers to buy something useless. I have to write. It's who I am.

So here I am, scanning the room for a place to sit. The way I see it, I have three options, and none of them are perfect.

I'd normally sit next to Michael, the gorgeous senior who continues to flirt with me. But, one, he writes like a *New York Times* reporter and, two, rumor has it he flirts with everybody. And I don't want to be "that" girl.

Second choice is a guy I've seen once or twice at the church my roommates and I go to *when* we get our Sunday morning act together. He has black curly hair, razor stubble that's kind of sexy, and olive skin hinting at exotic ancestry. Usually it would be fun to chat things up with him. He seems interesting, but I don't know his story. And since stories are how you're judged in this room, it's too risky.

The third, and easiest, choice would be to plop on the couch with the other sophomore, April. She's tiny, has shoulder-length, straight brown hair, large eyes, and a load of attitude. We've logged countless hours in the office working on edits together, and she always makes me laugh. We were assigned as critique partners in my freshman comp class. Let's just say her writing didn't wow me. And I don't want anyone here to assume my writing is the same caliber as hers. Which makes me wonder, why is she here? Did they invite all the sophomores to move up?

Focus, I remind myself.

"It's a risk." Michael's voice commands the room. "But I'm all about risks." He glances around, assessing his audience. He rests his eyes on mine for longer than a natural moment. "Palmer, you don't have a glass."

"Oh." My voice sounds tinny. I smile, noticing almost everyone else is holding a glass of wine. We don't do that in the English building. "I'm fine, thanks." I slide my silver cross pendant on its chain back and forth with an unsteady hand. I inhale and stand straighter, feet planted, muscles engaged, shoulders rolled back. My yoga instructor would be proud.

Instead of crumpling under Michael's steady gaze, I draw power from it, like a dare or an invitation. I take his opening and inch my way into the room with words. "Wasn't there talk about changing the name from Shamrock Saturday to Green Day?"

"I love their music, but they're not exactly news," April adds in her raspy voice. She shifts a few inches to the left on the couch, as if making room for me. It would be so easy to slide next to her. But she would lower my clout. Here, people are not assessed by looks, or money, or who their friends are. Here, we are judged by our craft. That scares the crap out of me. It also sharpens every one of my nerve endings.

"Dude, not the band. It's, like, the biggest event on campus." Brennan, a guy who mostly writes about the music scene, takes a hit of whatever he's smoking, something thick and foggy smelling, his eyes half closed under his shaggy bangs.

"It is big, but the university hates Shamrock Saturday and everything it stands for: drinking at 5:00 a.m., hundreds of drunks walking the streets all day dressed in green, and, oh yeah, the arrests," Summer says. "I heard that too, Palmer."

I nod. She knows my name. Good sign.

"President Downing thought it would make a statement if Shamrock Saturdays were history. Which could be an interesting lead into our coverage—can you squelch tradition with a name change?" Summer raises her wine glass to me in a kind of salute. Her glossy scarlet bob shifts on her shoulders as a smile forms on my lips.

Take that, Dad.

She continues, "This staff meeting might run awhile. Red or white?"

She knows my name and she's offering me wine. Really? I rock onto my heels to steady everything wobbly inside of me. I know all of the usual excuses—the tricks my roommates and I learned freshman year to avoid drinking when everyone else is—the "Oh, I'm on cold medicine and they don't mix" excuse. "I'm drinking water. Need to rehydrate after that intense workout today." Or "Someone's getting me a drink, thanks." But none of these make sense right now. I don't have a drink. No one else is getting me one. And if I mention being sick, I could look weak. Plus, wine seems kind of fun, sophisticated. I slide my cross on my chain again.

"You should at least try the Moscato," Michael whispers over my shoulder. He must have snuck around the room during my short interchange with Summer. "It's easy on the palate. A great starter wine. Sit tight."

"Thanks," I say, but I don't mean it. First, I don't want him or Summer or anyone else here to think I'm so immature I need "starter wine," whatever that means. But the truth is, I'm really not into the whole drinking thing. This circular argument makes my brain flip.

Stop.

I will the negative thoughts out of my head. *Chill,* I tell myself. Inhale. Exhale. One thing at a time. The wine.

There's nothing immoral about a college woman drinking one glass of wine. If anything, it's a sign of maturity and style. Wine is not the same thing as the beer bongs they sell at The Brewery, and Michael is pouring. And it looks like he grew out a beard over Christmas break. Very grown-up.

Summer sits next to Brennan on the chic leather couch. "The president's office has threatened the local T-shirt printers they'll yank all university orders if they print any shirts with references to beer or drunk leprechauns."

My roommates, Hannah, Kat, Claire, and I, would kill for that leather couch. We are sharing a dorm room again this year. It's a cute suite in Tomarken Hall, but I would love to have an apartment with hardwood floors instead of 1970's linoleum. I crave an actual kitchen instead of our mini fridge and Keurig. I barely hear the rest of what Summer says, I'm so busy mentally redecorating.

"I say we do it," Michael says, back at my side with a glass of honey-colored wine. He hands the stem to me and lets his fingers linger around mine as I take it. His touch is warm and inviting. Is he trying to tell me something? I can't be imagining that, can I? The glass is smooth and has a solid weight in my hand. I feel sophisticated swirling my bowl-shaped glass and letting the wine dance around the edges like a magic elixir.

I take a sip. The wine is strong but sweet. I let the thick, syrupy flavor roll across my tongue. It coats my throat with warmth. I take another.

From where he leans comfortably on the counter near me, Michael continues. "We can treat it like *60 Minutes*. You know, show both sides—why Clarkston doesn't approve, why the students do. We can do an interview on the street thing. Ask random people on the corner their opinion, snap their pictures, and use that as a sidebar." Michael's face becomes more and more animated as he talks. He has some sort of inner magnet that pulls the entire room toward him and what he has to say. "Ahmed, would you follow me around with your camera?" he asks.

"Sure." The dark, mysterious guy from church nods. That's Ahmed? I've seen his photo credits all over the magazine. I should have sat next to him. Why didn't I sit next to him?

"Or I could." Van, another photographer, bats her eyelashes. Her photos frequent the fashion page and restaurant reviews.

Gag. Blatant flirting. Is that allowed?

I want to say something brilliant, but I'm not sure if Summer wants to hear anything else from this newbie who might have been accidentally invited. But there's no point in being here if I'm not going to talk. I take a quick drink, as if my glass holds speaking potion instead of wine.

"What has *QuadAngles* done in the past few years on the topic?" I ask.

"Good question, Palmer." Summer elbows Brennan to keep him from nodding off, then continues, "Three years ago we tiptoed around Shamrock Saturday and wrote a St. Patrick's Day article that only mentioned Shamrock Saturday on a calendar listing of campus events. Two years ago we did nothing. Last year we did a story on all the positive events surrounding Shamrock Saturday—the Think Green recycling drive, the Green Mile race, and the green eggs and ham they serve at Murphy's. The president's office loved it."

"True. But all of those were sellouts." Michael steps forward and puts his hand on Summer's shoulder. She smiles. I stiffen. Michael and I have gone out to lunch twice to discuss some articles I was hoping to get in the magazine. Not that I'm counting. But he's never asked me *out* out.

"It's our job as journalists to explore the gritty, to go to the places no one else wants to go." He slides his arm off Summer's shoulder. I exhale. I notice she does too.

"Like the bathrooms of the Tipsy Toad?" Brennan laughs.

"Ew. Those are soooo gross. Definitely gritty." April scrunches her face and laughs. The only one who joins in is Brennan.

"Right." Summer stands and walks toward the stool where I'm perched. "Hey, that's not a bad idea." She paces back and forth clutching her iPad in one hand and her wine glass in the other. "You two"—she points to April and Brennan—"work on a one-pager on the ten best and ten worst restrooms on campus—include dorms, dining halls, book stores, bars, the works."

"Cool." April nods, her long beaded earrings swaying back and forth.

As Brennan and April argue over which downtown bar's bathrooms are the most disgusting, I flip through my journal.

"Please tell me you have some good ideas in there," Summer says, sighing and resting her chin on my shoulder.

"Well," I say. I turn my head to face her, hoping it diverts her eyes from my journal. My notes are poems, ideas, quotes, to-do lists, Bible verses, and ramblings, not content that would impress an editor. "I was thinking about a spring break guide. I know it's not original, but it could be if we highlighted some unique trips."

Stick a needle in my eye. How stupid can I sound? I should have sat next to April and gotten it over with.

"Spring break works." Summer glances at April and Brennan.

It does?

"Michael, why don't you take on the Shamrock Saturday article? Palmer, you'll work alongside him. Learn from him. Then show me what you've got with the spring break piece. A one-page spread with great images." Summer smiles, clinks my glass again, and says, "Welcome to the writing team."

"Thanks."

It's settled, then. I'm in.

"Cheers." Michael's glass nestles in the space between Summer's and mine so he can toast us simultaneously.

Death Cab for Cutie croons "I Will Follow You into the Dark" from the speakers, and the mood overtakes me. I would like to follow Michael, no doubt. I am surrounded by creative minds; writers and editors and photographers, bouncing ideas off each other, complimenting each other. I imagine this is what it was like for Hemingway and Fitzgerald in Paris in the 1920s.

I take another small sip. The wine is sweet and lingering, like Michael's touch.

Warmth spreads through me from the wine or the promotion, I am not sure which. My shoulders relax, and as Michael holds out the bottle offering more, I extend my glass toward him, feeling like I belong here.

TO KEEP READING ORDER IT'S ADDICTING

ACKNOWLEDGEMENTS

God, my creator, and the creator of my words—thank You for giving me this story and the chance to share it with others. May it find the hearts You seek.

Faye, Jodi, Laura and Michele—thank you for opening your hearts and sharing your stories. Your personal experiences of losing loved ones when they were too young to imagine them being gone formed Kat's thoughts, actions, and experiences. I will never be able to take away the pain from your losses, but hopefully Kat's story will help others know they are not alone.

Brett—my support, my rock, my true love. There is no me without you.

Max, Mallory, and Maguire—thank you for sweet notes on my white board, hugs, encouragement, and prayers for my writing. Our adventures together and your sweet love inspire me daily.

Maddie—thank you for teaching your nonathletic mom a thing or two about soccer. You gave Kat her kick!

Mom—thanks for all the stories you read to me as a girl and for the countless trips to the library. You taught me how to fall in love with books.

Julie Breihan—thank you for perfecting this story with your meticulous edits.

Laura Kurk, Jennifer Murgia, Stephanie Morrill, and Rajdeep Paulus—thank you for being my sisters of the traveling stories. You build me up and give my words wings.

Amy Parker—your belief in me fuels my writing. Your belief in Christ fuels my soul.

Tammy Bundy—a girl couldn't ask for a better writing twin. Thank you for always being there.

Birch House Press thank you for the beautiful home for my stories.

ABOUT THE AUTHOR

I believe in God. I believe in true love. I believe if I bang hard enough on the back of my wardrobe I'll get to Narnia someday. I believe eating chocolate is good for you. I believe part of my soul lives in France, part at the beach and the other part here in Oxford, Ohio, because when I go to those places I feel at home, as if I've always belonged. I believe heaven will feel much the same. I believe God created me to be the wife to my husband, the mother of my four kids, and to write stories He wanted to tell. My novels include It's Complicated, Skinny, Hot, It's Addicting and Angry.